A CURE IN THE WILD

A SAGE CANYON NOVEL

CARA DEVLIN

CHAPTER 1

Sage Canyon, Colorado
December 1901

*E*llie jerked awake at the crack of a gunshot. She stared into the darkened room, her pulse skipping in her neck.

A few seconds ago, she'd been in her family's sitting room in Boston, which was decorated from carpet to ceiling with the Christmas decorations her mother so loved: garlands and wreathes, red silk tapestries, mistletoe, a pair of jade mantle candlesticks only displayed in the month of December, and of course the enormous Balsam fir tree strung with ribbons and ornaments. The new wired lightbulbs Edison invented to take the place of small candles had been plugged in and shining.

Now, however, Ellie was in a small, dark room with only moonlight coming through the windows. The familiarity of her surroundings rushed over her, and she released a breath. She was at McClure's Tavern and Hotel. Boston was thousands of miles away. Sometimes, it felt like a whole world away. She certainly wouldn't have been jolted awake by the sound of gunshot in Boston.

Ellie flung back her quilt and sat up, setting her feet on the floor. She'd taken Audrey's advice at the end of November and now wore her wool stockings to bed each night. This would be Ellie's first "true" winter, Audrey had warned, and she would quickly learn ways to endure it. Audrey McClure, owner of McClure's and one of Ellie's dearest new friends, was a voice to heed. She'd raised her son here and had endured many long, snowy, frigid Colorado winters. If anyone knew how to make the best of the coming months, it would be Audrey.

As Ellie's heartbeat slowed and the patch of sweat on her chest began to cool, the fog of sleep lifted. Her dream of home faded like mist. There had been no people in her dream, just the room of holiday decorations. It had likely been in the forefront of her mind since reading Pearl's letter earlier that afternoon. Ellie's sister wrote every week or so, and the stack of her correspondence had grown to a formidable pile in her desk drawer. The letter from today had described their mother's traditional Christmas excitement and the transformation of their home, from the entrance hall to the dining room, the parlor and reading room, and each bedroom and guest room. Pearl had, once again, lamented that Ellie would not be home for Christmas this year, and Ellie's usual stab of guilt had deepened. It could not be helped. She simply couldn't hop onto a train and travel two thousand miles home for a visit. Especially not now.

As Sage Canyon's only physician, Ellie had responsibilities to her patients—the few of them that she possessed, anyway. She'd come to the small silver mining town in the Rocky Mountains in late September, accepting the position of town doctor from an advert in a newspaper back east. The timing had been ideal. The accidental death of a boy in Ellie's care at Children's Hospital had left her reputation as a doctor in tatters, and after months of humiliation, scandal, and self-doubt—and the dissolution of her engagement to the best catch in Boston—Ellie had come to the realization that she would never again be welcome to practice medicine in Boston, or likely anywhere else in the east.

Even with her woolen stockings, the cold floor reached into her feet as she went to the windows overlooking Main Street. She'd become used to the view from her room at McClure's, though she wasn't usually awake at so early an hour. The clock, brightened by a ray of moonlight, read only three. Goodness, even Audrey wouldn't be awake for another two hours to begin breakfast. As she stood at the window, staring out into the street, Ellie began to wonder if the gunshot had merely been part of her dream. Though, she wasn't sure what the report of a gun would be doing in her cozy Christmas memory.

The snow on the ground had to be at least a foot deep. It started the evening before, coming down from the gray sky in sideways drifts. There had already been a few snowstorms since the start of November, and though Ellie was used to snow, having lived her whole life in the northeast, she'd been surprised at just how quickly the snow piled up here. It was almost as if the clouds ripped apart, dumped their loads in vicious heaps, and then sealed up again and moved along. Hours later, the sun would come out and melt it all in a snap. Though for some reason, the snowfall tonight felt different. It was colder. Ice rimmed her window. It didn't look like the snow would be going anywhere, perhaps for days.

She sighed and let the curtain fall back into place. The gunshot was probably nothing. A homesteader had likely caught a coyote sneaking around a chicken coop. Ellie went to the potbelly stove. What had been a leaping fire before she'd gone to bed had all but snuffed out. With practiced motions, she opened the door and heaved in a few more pieces of wood from the box at her feet.

Caleb, Audrey's son, filled the box every afternoon, and he'd even left her a pair of sturdy canvas work gloves so that she wouldn't give herself a splinter when lifting the logs to feed the stove. He was a thoughtful young man, and in the few months since Ellie had come to Sage Canyon, he'd slowly started to speak more around her. Caleb still hardly looked her in the eye, his painfully shy manner a product of his natural personality. She'd heard unkind whispers from some of the miners Audrey served each night at supper, calling Caleb "idiot" or "retarded," but Ellie had met several children back in Boston with the same sort of personality, and none of them had been unintelligent. Caleb certainly wasn't either.

She shut the stove door and hurried back to her bed, pulling the quilt up around her again. Audrey and Caleb had given her a welcoming sense of home at McClure's, as did Maggie, their hired girl. But there were moments, like this one, when Ellie felt entirely alone. When she wondered if coming so far west, to this tiny mining town, had been a good decision.

A shiver rumbled its way down her spine and out along her arms as she laid in bed, unblinking. There was no sound except for the soft and steady *tink tink* of snowy ice against her window. But then came a cough and the rattle and creak of the frozen porch steps. Someone had stepped up onto them. A fist pounded on the front door to McClure's.

Ellie sat up. She leaped out of bed and immediately went to her closet. There was no reason for anyone to come calling at McClure's at three in the morning unless it was an emergency. *This has to do with the gunshot.*

She took out her heavy cloak and boots, and her hat, mittens, and scarf as whoever it was pounded on the door yet again, and Audrey could be heard answering it. Before anyone could come upstairs to fetch her, Ellie wrapped herself up and grabbed her black leather doctor's bag, which she kept on the trunk at the foot of her bed.

She met Audrey on the stairs. Her friend's robe was drawn tightly against her throat, her long, dark hair still in wrappers.

"What's happened?" Ellie asked.

"Frank Eberly," she answered breathlessly as she led Ellie down to the darkened front hall. "He's been shot."

"Is he at The Canary?"

She'd found the older man at Sage Canyon's only saloon once with a bleeding head and split lip after a bar brawl. Then again, on second thought, The Canary probably wouldn't be open at this hour.

A man stood in the middle of Audrey's front hall. Snow dusted the tops of his shoulders, and he'd tracked it in, onto the rug, too. He whipped off his hat, his white-blond hair gleaming in the glow of Audrey's single hurricane lamp. Blood streaked his cheek and chin.

Ellie pulled back. "Mr. Walker."

Nate Walker had captured the heart of Frank Eberly's daughter, Myra, and much to Frank's fury and disapproval, had wed her earlier in October. The young man wasn't well liked in town in general, considering he'd once ridden with the Hodge brothers —a gang that had terrorized the area a few years before. However, lately he was trying to turn over a new leaf. His bride had all the faith in the world in him, and Ellie was inclined toward giving him a second chance as well.

"Frank's got a bullet to the gut," he said now, slapping his hat back on.

Dread poured into her chest. "Where is he?" she asked, following him as he opened the front door and stepped onto the porch.

"At the store."

Frank owned a silver prospecting store in town. He hadn't allowed Ellie to treat him that time at the saloon, but a gunshot wound might change his mind.

"Is he conscious?"

The drifts of snow on the porch reached her shins. Ellie couldn't even see the porch steps and was thankful to have Nate's boot prints to step into on the way down.

"He wasn't when I left to get you," he called back. "Myra's with him."

There was no more time to talk, or energy for that matter. On the street, the snow was up to Ellie's kneecaps. It wasn't a powdery, light snowfall either but a heavier, icy mix. They lifted their legs to trudge through it, their feet coming down like pistons in a machine, propelling them forward. Ellie kept her chin tucked, the brim of her hat shielding the whipping snow from her eyes. But the sharp flakes still managed to catch on her lashes, making it a challenge to see Nate just ahead of her. As if being in the dark and the driving snow wasn't menacing enough, she also anticipated a patient with a bullet in his stomach.

It would be a tricky, possibly hopeless wound.

What had happened, who had shot him, and why were all questions that cluttered Ellie's mind, but more important to her right now was the treatment required to save Frank Eberly's life. She had the instruments and materials in her doctor's bag to assist her with whatever procedure she'd need to perform, but... the question of *if* she could do it rose up like a black storm cloud over her head. Like these very real clouds, this black one seemed to split open and dump pure ice down her back.

Her first night in Sage Canyon felt like ages ago now, but it had been somewhat similar. She'd been soaking in the copper tub at Audrey's after her long journey west when gunshots had sounded. When Ellie had gotten dressed and emerged from the washroom, a wounded man had been sitting in Audrey's front parlor.

Jack Granger. The thought of him warmed Ellie as she lumbered along behind Nate Walker. The man had exasperated her from the moment they'd met outside The Silver Strike in Grantstown, the afternoon she'd arrived in Colorado. Just a few miles down the tracks from Sage Canyon, Grantstown was larger, wealthier, and more populated. Her train had stopped to deliver most of its passengers before continuing on to the terminus of Sage Canyon, Ellie its sole remaining passenger. She'd seen two men fighting outside a saloon, and one had fallen with a blow to the head. Unable to look the other way, Ellie had rushed to inspect the unconscious man's head—only to have the barrel of a pistol stuck between her ribs as thanks.

As soon as Jack realized she was a woman and not a pickpocket, he'd holstered his piece, but the first impression had been made. Later that same night, when he'd arrived with a gunshot wound to his shoulder, the impression had firmly cemented. However, over the next few weeks, Ellie slowly came to realize Jack Granger wasn't just a troublemaker. He was the town's ex-sheriff, a grieving widower, and one of the most kind-hearted men she had ever met.

As the glow of lamplight from Eberly's Prospecting suddenly appeared through the snowstorm, Ellie recalled the relative ease of Jack's shoulder wound. Frank's would be anything but easy.

Inside the shop, she was met with a scene that instantly seared itself into her mind: Frank, on the floor, covered with a blanket. His daughter, Myra, kneeling behind him, resting his head on her lap. By her glassy, red-rimmed eyes, it was clear she'd been crying, but now, she only wore a solemn, flat expression.

One look at Frank Eberly and Ellie knew it was too late.

His eyes were closed, likely pressed into that position by Myra, and his lips were slack. Even though she was certain he was dead, Ellie knelt at his side, pulled off her glove, and felt for a pulse. A handful of seconds later, she retracted her hand, feeling a swooping sensation in the pit of her stomach.

"I'm so sorry, Myra."

The young woman's nostrils flared, and her chin quivered. She nodded her head, and then shifted her father's head from her lap. Nate gently pulled her up, into an embrace. Myra wrapped her arms around her middle. She wasn't far enough along to be showing, but Ellie had heard the happy news just last week that they were expecting a child in the summer.

Ellie looked away. A sharp pang of longing surprised her in that horrible moment. It had been some time since Jack had held her like that. Shaking away the untimely and inappropriate thought, she peeled back the woolen blanket that had been draped over Frank's body. She grimaced at the sight of so much blood. His hands were covered with it, from where he'd gripped the wound.

"What happened, Myra? Nate?" she asked after giving them a few moments.

Myra swiped at her wet cheeks as she turned out of her new husband's embrace. "I don't know, exactly. I was upstairs, asleep —or trying to fall back asleep, at least."

"I'd gone down to the wood stove to put in a few more logs," Nate explained.

In the middle of the shop, a cast iron wood stove looked practically cold. Next to it was a box of kindling and a stack of roughly cut logs.

"I heard voices out back," he went on, nodding toward the door behind the counter that led to a back room.

"Someone was with Frank?" Ellie asked.

"The shot went off before I could feed the stove. By the time I got into his room, the back door was wide open, and Frank…" His eyes settled on his father-in-law. "He was struggling."

Myra closed her eyes and swayed. Nate tightened his hold on her. There had been a lot of tension between the two of them and Frank for some time. Mostly, it had to do with the fact that Frank had thought nothing of raising a hand to his daughter when she'd fallen in love with the ex-criminal. He'd also been a drunk and a thoroughly unpleasant man. Ellie peered down at his body. No matter what he'd been in life, he hadn't deserved to be murdered.

The staggering thought made her shiver. The fireless stove and the snow that had slipped into her boots on the way to the shop made it worse. Frank Eberly had been *murdered*.

She met Myra's eyes. Then Nate's. "We need to fetch the sheriff."

"I'll go," Nate said, but Myra held his arm when he tried to step away.

"But he's not in town, remember?"

And suddenly, Ellie did. Sheriff Payton had stopped by Audrey's the afternoon before to let her know that he'd be leaving Charlie Munns in charge while he went to Denver on family business. His father had passed away, and he needed to take care of arrangements. He'd been stoic about it, but Ellie had noticed his hands tremble as Audrey pressed a cup of coffee into them. The sheriff was a good man. Young and serious and by-the-book.

Who would have imagined a murder would unfold while he was away?

"Then fetch Deputy Munns," Ellie said, and with a nod, Nate went back out into the storm. Ellie crouched to pull the blanket up over Frank's face. Gooseflesh riddled her arms and legs, and her toes were painful blocks of ice.

"Myra, why don't you feed the stove?" It would keep her busy, at least.

As she went to the stove to occupy herself with the much-needed chore, Ellie eyed the open door behind the counter again. Someone had shot Frank and then fled. Perhaps there would be a trail of boot prints. She went to the room and peered inside. Her few times inside the shop, she'd assumed it was an office of sorts, and it was, but it was also Frank's living quarters. The newly wedded Walkers had taken the upstairs rooms. Living with her father even after being married had been Myra's choice—she was used to caring for him, especially when he became inebriated. And as much as Frank had grumbled annoyance to anyone who would listen, he'd allowed the bride and groom to make their home above the shop.

Frank's room was arctic, the outside door still open. A huge drift of snow had blown inside, over the floor, and more drifted in, gusting with such force the curtains on the opposite side of the room fluttered in a mad dance. Blood speckled the floor and a threadbare rug on the way toward the shop's front room, where Frank now rested.

Ellie stepped around the blood on her way to the snow drifts. If there had been boot prints left behind, they were now buried by snow. She shut the door after a brief struggle with the pile-up and then inspected the surroundings. A candle flickered on a desk across the room, next to a slim bed. Frank had likely lit it when he'd had his midnight caller.

Ellie rubbed her arms and shivered. She'd dealt with death plenty of times before, but never a murder. Sage Canyon was small though. Someone was sure to know who might be to blame.

She started for the front of the shop but came to an abrupt stop in the open doorway. Myra was no longer feeding logs into the stove but standing over her father's covered figure. She stared down at him with a look of such loathing that Ellie's breath caught. Her nostrils were flared, and one eyebrow was arched high. The grimace on Myra's lips nearly looked like a twisted half-grin.

She glanced up at Ellie. "I hated him sometimes."

Ellie slowly made her way forward, cautious.

"Myra—" she started to say, but the door blasted open, and in stumbled Deputy Munns, Nate, and to Ellie's utter surprise, a snow-cloaked Jack Granger.

"What are you doing here?" she blurted.

He took off his hat and knocked the snow from the brim. His grin wasn't as sly as usual, but it managed to heat her cheeks and inform her on how rude she'd sounded.

"Good to see you too, doc."

CHAPTER 2

$\mathcal{D}$eputy Munns approached the blanketed figure on the floor. He doffed his hat swiftly and met Ellie's eyes, looking ashamed that he hadn't thought to take off his hat as soon as he'd stepped inside the shop. His bright red cheeks were wet from the storm, his boot tips peaked with snow.

"Walker says it was an intruder?" he asked, his eyes skipping between Ellie and Myra.

"That's right," Myra answered.

Ellie thought of the open back door, the drifts of snow. She hadn't seen prints, but then again, it wouldn't have taken long for snow to bury them. Her own prints from here to McClure's were likely filled in already.

"Doc?" Jack stepped up beside her. He carried the cold in on his coat, along with the smell of woodsmoke and tobacco. Ellie frowned, wondering why he wasn't at his ranch, just outside of town.

"Walker said it was a shot to his gut?" he continued.

"I haven't had the opportunity to do a thorough examination, but yes, that's what it looks like."

She realized then that she would be required to do a postmortem. Her pulse sputtered. She'd never done one before and having known the deceased in life would make it strange, indeed.

"Show me where it happened, Walker," Jack said, and again, Ellie wondered at his presence.

He'd been sheriff of Sage Canyon for many years before he lost the job to his own deputy, Payton. After his wife's murder, Jack had become obsessed with tracking down the Hodge gang and seeing them all tossed in jail—or strung up. It didn't matter to him, so long as they were arrested and stopped.

Jack had admitted to losing sight of his duty to the town, of drinking too much and letting too many things slide. He was no longer effective as sheriff and so, after a number of complaints, the governor took his badge and handed it over to Payton. It had been a dark time for him, made worse by the absence of his beloved wife.

However, since then, Jack's fury had tempered. And when, just a few months ago, he'd had the opportunity to have Nate Walker arrested for a crime the young man hadn't committed, he'd taken the high road. He didn't like Nate Walker, but Jack knew his wife had been killed by another Hodge gang member's gun, not Nate's. He'd finally let go of his hatred for him.

Now, the two men walked toward Frank's room while Deputy Munns crouched and pulled back the blanket. A visible shiver worked its way down his spine, and he dropped the blanket as he would a burning coal. Ellie had only made the deputy's acquaintance a few times, but she got the impression that he wasn't in the least bit comfortable with corpses.

Within the next hour, as the sun reached over the peaks of the twin mountains cradling the mining town, the shop became a hub of activity. Audrey arrived, having trudged through the dwindling storm with a carafe of coffee and warm, honeyed biscuits. She'd taken charge of Myra, shuttling her upstairs to get dressed and away from the gritty business unfolding in the shop.

After informing Munns and Jack of all that he knew of the

intrusion and the killing, Nate found a wood plank. He fashioned a makeshift cot, and then he and Jack carried Frank's body across the street to Ellie's infirmary. She followed, relieved to be gone from the prospecting shop. Her infirmary was like a second home, tucked at the end of a wide alleyway next to the saloon. At first, Jack had been skeptical of her working so close to The Canary, but the saloon hadn't proven to be as much of a den of sin as it was simply loud and sometimes busy.

The owner, Dade, rented out the infirmary for a fair monthly fee. Ellie would often find him lounging in the open connecting door to the saloon with a ready story about his customers, a question about what she was doing, or something insignificant, like a tale about how a particular bullet in the wall had come to be lodged there. While she didn't mind his presence most of the time, this morning, she wished he'd slept in.

He must have heard the commotion as Ellie unlocked the infirmary door, allowing Jack and Nate to enter with the cot. Either that, or he'd seen them coming down Green Street, struggling through the heaps of snow while balancing Frank's body. Dade knocked on the connecting door before unlocking it with the key he possessed. Ellie sighed.

"Dade, this isn't a good time."

His eyes stuck to the plank and the covered body laid out on top of it. "I know that bald head," he said, referring to the exposed pate.

"You would. Frank passed out on your bar nearly every night," Jack said as he and Nate lowered the plank onto the patient table.

Over the last few months, the infirmary had gradually filled up with supplies and furnishings, and it now appeared just as Ellie had pictured possible. Although few in number, her patients felt comfortable in the space with its silk screen privacy panels, warm rugs, a landscape painting on each wall, and even a cheery bouquet of yellow paper roses that Katherine Toft, the mercantile owner, had surprised Ellie with a week ago.

This was, however, the first time a dead body had graced the patient table.

"Was Frank at The Canary last night?" Jack asked as he pulled back the blanket to expose Frank's face.

"Wasn't he every night?" Dade replied.

"Alone?"

"As always. Can't blame anyone for not wanting to listen to his bellyaching."

"What was he complaining about last night?" Jack asked.

Dade shrugged. "The usual. Money, the weather, his lump of a son-in-law—no offense, Walker."

Nate grimaced but made no reply.

"He didn't argue with anyone?" Jack pressed.

"Just himself. Delusional grumbling. Seemed to think the sheriff was still in town and wanted to throw him in jail for something." Dade furrowed his brow. "You investigating, Granger?"

Ellie glanced over her shoulder as she opened the supply cabinet and searched Jack's face for a reaction. His strong jaw tensed.

"Just trying to find out what happened," he replied.

"This have anything to do with the gunshot I heard a few hours back?" Dade asked.

Ellie turned to Dade, her hands full of linens and a jar of carbolic acid. "You heard it, too?"

It shouldn't have surprised her. The Canary was closer to the prospecting shop than McClure's.

"Couldn't sleep with all that wind," he muttered.

"Did you look outside when you heard the shot?" Ellie asked. "Perhaps see something?"

Dade arched a brow. "Couldn't see past the front porch, the snow was so thick."

Ellie's cheeks heated. Of course. She should have thought of that, considering she'd trudged through it on the way to the shop.

"Gentlemen," she said, "I'll conduct the postmortem now, if you don't mind."

She needed a quiet room for that.

Dade looked a little green as he slipped back into the saloon and closed the door. Nate Walker slid his hat back on his head and backed up as well. Ellie could tell he wanted to return to Myra as soon as possible. Her heart swelled at Nate's obvious affection for his new wife.

"Would you mind if I stayed?" Jack asked as soon as Nate slipped out the door.

Ellie's stomach cinched tight. "Stay?"

She'd never performed a postmortem before, and having Jack watch her on her first one gave her an unexpected case of jitters.

"I can go if you'd rather that," he said, hitching a thumb toward the door, one of his half-grins forming.

She *would* rather be alone for this first procedure...but she also wasn't eager for Jack to leave. It had been nearly a week since she'd last seen him, and while the circumstances of tonight's meeting were less than ideal, she had to admit his arrival at Eberly's had given her some comfort. If she could have, she would have leaned into him the way Myra had with Nate. But while there had been a few stolen kisses the last two months, everything between her and Jack still felt awkward and new.

"I... No, you can stay. If you'll assist?"

If he was at work, it might make her less uneasy.

Ellie started to remove her jacket and belatedly remembered that she was still wearing a nightdress. Audrey had given her the thick flannel gown in November when she'd found Ellie in the kitchen one night making tea. The one Ellie was wearing had been made of thin linen, and while the lace cuffs, hem, and neckline were beautiful, it was also a far cry from warm. Audrey had seen her standing next to the stove, shoulders wrapped in a shawl, hands rubbing together for friction, and had started chuckling. The next evening, Ellie found a lovely blue-and-white checked flannel gown with a high collar and long sleeves, cinched at the wrists with ribbon, folded on the trunk at the foot of her bed.

Now, she was more grateful than ever that Audrey had left it for her. She couldn't even begin to imagine the embarrassment of finding herself in a thin white nightdress in front of Jack. He rubbed the back of his neck and, with a bashful grin, averted his eyes.

"I didn't have time to change," Ellie explained.

He only grinned wider, mischievously peeking up at her. She yanked down her pinafore hanging on a peg and threw it on, tying the ribbons at the back.

"What can I do?" Jack asked, removing his own jacket and rolling up his sleeves. His hat was already on Ellie's desk, the worn brown Stetson nearly black from the wet snow.

Ellie instructed him to go out back and pump some water from the well, and meanwhile, she removed the blanket from Frank's body and began the task of undressing him. It was more than a little uncomfortable, considering she'd been acquainted with him, however fractionally, in life. But she soon found the focus she needed and fell into the familiar rhythm of assessing the patient—or corpse, in this case—in her care.

"A single gunshot to the abdomen," she said after inspecting him. "No exit wound. No other injuries are apparent. No bruises, scratches, any kind of evidence of a struggle."

Ellie noted the blackened area around the wound, as did Jack.

"He was shot close range," he said. "That's soot from the muzzle."

Ellie cleaned away what she could of the residue, but there was still a charred halo around the wound.

"The muzzle burned his skin when the gun discharged," he said.

"So, the shooter had to have pressed the pistol into his stomach," Ellie determined.

"Frank let him get close." Jack frowned. "Now, why would he do that?"

Ellie added the observations to her notes—she would most certainly need to supply them to Sheriff Payton when he returned, and perhaps even the regional police office in Grantstown.

"Frank must have known his assailant," she murmured.

What Myra had said in the moments before Nate returned with Jack and Deputy Munns flickered to the front of her mind, as did the expression she'd worn when looking down on her father's body. One of such loathing, it had made the hairs on Ellie's arms stand on end.

"What is it?" Jack asked.

Ellie realized she'd stopped scratching notes and was just staring at the paper.

Myra had said she'd hated him sometimes, but that didn't mean anything, did it? Ellie didn't know her very well, but she didn't seem capable of such a crime. Besides, why would she choose to shoot her father now? She was happily married, and Nate would never have allowed Frank to raise a hand to her, the way he used to.

"Doc?" Jack stepped closer. Touched her elbow. "You okay?"

She blinked and set down the pencil. If she mentioned Myra's comment or anything about that expression, Jack would march right over to Eberly's and begin questioning her. He might not be sheriff but there was no doubt he still maintained authority in Sage Canyon. Myra had already been through enough.

"I'm fine." Ellie tucked a stray curl of hair behind her ear. "It's just…this is my first postmortem, and I wish it didn't have to be on someone I was acquainted with."

It was a good enough excuse, mostly because it wasn't a lie.

"I understand. Frank was a sonofabitch—pardon me," he said quickly. "But he didn't deserve this."

Ellie didn't mind Jack swearing. He always apologized, as if ashamed he'd cussed in front of a lady. He was chivalrous and protective, and whenever he held Ellie's gaze for longer than was necessary, she felt trapped between wanting to boldly hold his stare and look away shyly.

Now, however, Jack's eyes rested on the body laid out on her examination table. She felt absurd and guilty thinking about Jack romantically when they were in such a somber situation.

She got her head on straight and dove back into the procedure, using a pair of needle nose forceps to find the slug, which was lodged near the spine.

"With a shot like that, he didn't suffer, at least," Jack said as she dropped the flattened lead bullet into a bowl of water.

Ellie's stomach cramped as she sutured the incision. When she'd gone to bed last night, she'd anticipated waking up to a snow globe world with nothing to do but have tea and breakfast in Audrey's kitchen—and perhaps shovel the front porch with Caleb. Not this.

"What now?" Ellie asked as she began to wash the body. "Will Deputy Munns handle the investigation until Sheriff Payton returns?"

The sheriff hadn't been specific about when he'd get back, just that he might be a few weeks.

Jack reached into the bowl and picked up the slug. "I'm sure he will."

He didn't sound confident, however, and recalling the timid way the deputy had handled himself at the prospecting shop, Ellie wasn't certain Munns was up to the task. If she felt that way, most likely others did as well. Jack included.

"What were you doing in town so early?" Ellie asked as she worked, sparing Jack a quick glance.

He shrugged. "Figured Munns might need help come morning after a storm. Last year, a few roofs collapsed during a blizzard, and a man got lost between his house and barn—got turned around and wandered for a mile. Nearly froze to death."

Without Sheriff Payton present, he wanted to lend a hand. Ellie bit back a grin.

"You're still sheriff at heart, aren't you?"

Jack eyed her with an arch of his brow and no smile. "You know that's over and done with. I'm just a concerned citizen." He placed the bullet in the small breast pocket of his vest. "I'll bring this to Munns, if that's all right."

Ellie nodded, intuition telling her not to push the subject. Jack Granger was a natural lawman even if he didn't want to admit it.

He'd been relieved of his duty at the darkest time in his life. Maybe he hadn't been fit for duty then, when he was still struggling with the senseless loss of his wife and the need for justice that seemed just out of his reach. But he was better now. At least Ellie thought he was. There was still a bleak sadness about him every now and then, though. Ellie caught sight of it when Jack didn't think anyone was looking at him. Losing Sarah had been devastating. Too devastating to ever truly recover? To open his heart and let someone else in? These were the questions Ellie had wondered countless times over the last few months. She also suspected it was the reason their relationship hadn't progressed much past a declaration of caring for each other, and chaste, brief kisses.

Jack opened the infirmary door and tugged on his hat. "Someone will come for the body soon. You'll be all right here?"

She couldn't imagine why she wouldn't be, but that didn't stop her from wishing Jack would stay. It was ridiculous, and totally unbecoming, to long for his company when she had this somber business to see to. Ellie quickly nodded and said, "Of course," and then Jack shut the door behind him.

The quiet gave her more room to work efficiently. She finished washing Frank and then with a slight struggle, redressed him. It was then that she realized he had been fully dressed when shot. Trousers, shirt, union suit, stockings, even jacket. Her own father usually wore a pair of silk pajamas to bed, but he was a United States Senator and could afford such a luxury. She doubted Frank had seen anything made of silk in the whole of his life.

Frowning, she wondered why he had been fully dressed at three in the morning. Unless he'd passed out drunk before he could strip to his union suit. However, another realization struck: not once had she smelled the lingering traces of spirits on him. Perhaps he hadn't been drunk after all. She would have to ask Dade the next time she saw him; going to the saloon right then to question him felt like an insurmountable task.

Finished with her postmortem at last, she sat behind her desk and put together her notes for the coroner or the marshal or whomever Deputy Munns contacted in Grantstown. At least Jack had the bullet slug; he'd be able to determine the type of pistol used. Perhaps, as he and Munns questioned more people in town, they could narrow down who it might have been.

It made her uneasy, glancing up and seeing the body under the white sheet. Relief loosened her limbs when Nate and two other men arrived about an hour later to take the body.

"How is Myra feeling?" Ellie asked.

"She'll be all right," Nate answered as he opened the door for the two other men carrying the litter.

"And the baby? I know she isn't very far along, but I wondered if she'd be coming in to see me soon."

Nate shifted onto the porch, his eyes skipping away from hers. "She'll be seeing Tamora, doc. I hope you don't take any offense. It's just…she's known around here for her midwifing."

Disappointment burned in Ellie's chest, but she forced a grin. "No offense taken. But if she should need anything…" She trailed off, knowing it was pointless.

Tamora had been in Sage Canyon far longer than Ellie and was indeed known for her midwifery skills. She'd also served as nurse and physician before Ellie arrived, which made getting her own foothold here in town a challenge. In fact, even though she and Tamora had found their way to appreciating their very different methods—Tamora applied folk medicine, whereas Ellie relied on modern advancements and techniques, or what Tamora called "institutional medicine"—it was up to the townspeople themselves to decide who they wished to see when they were sick or, like Myra, with child.

Being a woman physician and new to town had been two strikes against her, however it was the third strike that had all but ruined Ellie. When the mayor and his wife learned about Todd Andrews, the boy Ellie accidentally overdosed on morphine in Boston, they made sure the entire town knew too. While she had some understanding friends and patients willing to overlook her past, the vast majority of Sage Canyon still kept their distance.

As discouraging as it was, Ellie couldn't fault them. Her mistake had made her question everything about herself, even if she should be practicing medicine at all. But she loved what she did, and she hated giving up, giving in. The idea of quitting turned her inside out. Besides, if she did quit medicine, she wanted it to be *her* decision. She couldn't stand the thought of anyone else making it for her.

As soon as Nate and his helpers were gone, and the infirmary was relieved of its heavy burden, exhaustion swept over her from crown to foot. It was only mid-morning and yet Ellie felt ready for one of Audrey's hearty suppers and then a long night's rest.

An appropriate dress would also be nice.

She quickly put on her jacket, covering her nightdress, and then pulled on her hat. Taking up her doctor's bag, she flipped the sign in the front window to *"Closed: Find Me at McClure's."*

CHAPTER 3

There were a couple other boarding houses in Sage Canyon, but McClure's was the finest, by far. Ellie had considered renting a space of her own a few months ago with rooms upstairs to live and a space downstairs for the infirmary. If it hadn't been for the swift decline in patients after the Boston scandal was made known, she might have decided to do it. But she'd made a promise to herself when she'd left Boston against her parents' wishes: She would earn her keep and not be beholden to them or their money. A simple wire sent back east would infuse her bank account at the Grantstown Extension Savings and Loan, but she didn't want to have to stoop to it. Coming west had been a risk, but it had been her risk. Asking her father for money would be admitting defeat.

Ellie trudged through the heavy, wet snow as she made her way up Main Street. Her boots were soaked, her hem too, and the snow drifts in some places were up to her knees. The sun shone brightly, and already, icicles hanging from roof overhangs were dripping a steady stream as they melted.

"Doc Ellie!"

She looked up at the shout and squinted against the sunlight.

With a hand to shade her eyes, she saw Katherine Toft on the front steps of the mercantile store. The young woman waved madly at her.

"Come quickly!" she shouted before disappearing back into the store.

Ellie picked up her trudging pace. Katherine had taken over the reins at the store when her father, Barry Toft, had been shot and injured in the same shootout that had killed Jack's wife. A bullet lodged too closely to Mr. Toft's spine and the shoddy operation performed by the town's old doctor had ended up paralyzing him.

Ellie had only seen him a few times in the months she'd been in Sage Canyon and never for a proper meeting. He didn't like to be around people anymore, Katherine had explained. The wheeled chair he was confined to humiliated him.

Now, as Ellie's heart raced and perspiration dampened her skin from the struggle through the mounds of snow, she wondered if something had happened to him.

She finally made it to the front steps and with aching legs, climbed them. She burst through the door, panting.

"I told you, I don't need help!" was the shrill greeting she received.

Sitting on the floor in the middle of the mercantile was one of Ellie's least favorite people in town. Muriel Carson, the mayor's wife, was nearly spitting fire at Katherine Toft, who kneeled beside her. Muriel speared Ellie with a glare. "Your services are neither needed nor wanted."

Had the harsh words come from anyone else, Ellie might have been knocked back on her heels. But Muriel Carson's dislike for the town physician was no new thing, and quite honestly, Ellie matched it with her own dislike for Muriel.

She quickly assessed the way the mayor's wife sat with one leg out straight and the other bent at the knee, her hand resting on the ankle.

"Did you twist it?" Ellie asked.

Muriel turned her vehement glare onto Katherine next. "The front steps weren't shoveled properly."

Katherine bit her inner cheek to keep from responding, but Ellie could see the desire burning in her eyes.

"Why don't we get Mrs. Carson a chair to sit in?" Ellie said, reaching for her arm. But, as expected, she batted the helping hand away.

"I am not an invalid," she hissed, and with ungainly motions, got herself to her feet, wincing as she applied weight to her injured ankle.

"I'd like to make sure it isn't broken," Ellie said, determined not to let the woman get underneath her skin. Ellie was a physician, and as such, she had a duty to offer assistance to anyone who needed it—even bitter, sharp-tongued adversaries.

"I would know if it were broken," she retorted, limping toward the door. "Now, I find that I don't need anything at all in this store that I can't get on my next trip to Grantstown. Good day, Miss Toft."

She limped out the door, and though she didn't bid Ellie a farewell, she did level a cutting glare before slamming the door behind her. Muriel hobbled down the steps. A second later, there came a thumping noise and a shriek. Ellie and Katherine gaped at each other before rushing to the door. Through the long twin panes, they saw Muriel Carson brushing off her rump, which was once again plastered with snow.

"She left before I could shovel *properly*," Katherine said, a snort of laughter slipping out.

Ellie covered her own smile with her hand, and they quickly moved away from the front door's windows so they wouldn't be seen.

"Oh, that woman!" Ellie sighed. "I'm starting to think she hates me more with every passing day."

The potbelly wood stove in the center of Toft's pumped out

heat, the flames leaping behind the grated door. Ellie drifted toward it, her boots cold and wet, her frozen feet feeling nearly atrophied.

"What she really hates is that you stayed in Sage Canyon instead of running off with your tail between your legs, like she wanted you to. Like she promised you would," Katherine replied as she went behind the front counter. "She truly hates being wrong."

Katherine poured coffee from a tin percolator into a mug and came back around the counter to press it into Ellie's hands. "I'm sorry I dragged you all the way over here to look at her ankle. The way she was fussing, I worried it was broken."

The mug was almost too hot for Ellie to hold, but she let the heat seep into her cold hands and loosen the stiff tendons and muscles.

"Don't apologize, I was just making my way back to Audrey's." She sipped the coffee, peeking out over the brim. "It's been a long morning."

Katherine's grin fell. "I heard. Everyone's been saying Frank was shot dead, but no one seems to know more than that."

She took another long sip of coffee, suddenly wondering what she should or shouldn't share. Frank Eberly hadn't been her patient, not truly, so it wasn't the divulging of confidential information that held her back. It was the fact that this was a crime. Ellie was certain there were details she shouldn't gossip about with townsfolk.

"I'm afraid I don't know much more either," Ellie said.

Katherine took a deep breath. "What horrible timing for the sheriff to be in Denver. Are there any plans to wire him?"

"I'm sure Deputy Munns will." The steam warmed her cold nose and chin, but it did nothing to cure her cold, aching feet.

"The marshal is in Grantstown," Katherine offered.

"I suppose Munns might contact him. Though, I'm not sure there's even a suspect at this point." Letting that little detail be known wouldn't cause any harm. She certainly wasn't going to confide in Katherine about the strange thing Myra had said, or the cold expression she wore when gazing at her dead father's body. It still bothered her, no matter how she tried to reason it away or not think of it.

"Marshal Bevins is from back east, too," Katherine said while waving to customers as the brass bell rung them in. "Washington, D.C., I believe."

"Is that so." Ellie wondered if Katherine had told her that for any particular reason. She waited for her say something more and was rewarded for it.

"The truth is, he and Jack Granger don't much like one another."

The mention of Jack's name lit her interest. Not for the first time, she wondered if the mention of her name sparked the same interest in him.

Katherine continued, "After the shootout that killed Sarah, the marshal had to step in whenever Jack would disappear for weeks on end, hunting down the Hodge gang. And when Jack finally turned up, they'd practically come to blows." She lowered her voice and faced away from the other shoppers in the store. "It was Marshal Bevins who asked the governor to revoke his badge."

Back at the infirmary, Jack had insisted he'd put those hard times behind him. That he'd moved on. Ellie suspected it wasn't entirely true. Losing his badge had been a felling blow. He'd already lost his wife. Next, he'd lost his position—his purpose— in Sage Canyon.

Ellie wondered why he'd bothered to stay. When she'd lost everything back in Boston, she'd only wanted to disappear. Clearly, Jack was made of stronger stuff.

She took one last sip of coffee. "Then I suppose it's a good thing Deputy Munns will be dealing with the marshal." Ellie handed the mug back. "Thanks, Katherine. Oh, and how is your father?"

Katherine's sad, chagrined smile was commonplace whenever Ellie asked after Barry Toft. She still felt wretched that it had been her father who discovered Ellie's scandalous past through one of the Boston newspapers he subscribed to. He was so mistrustful of doctors with sullied reputations that he'd wanted to warn the whole town, starting with Mayor Carson.

"The cold weather seems to get into his bones, but he's doing well enough," Katherine answered. "I keep asking him if he'll allow an introduction, but..." She stopped and shrugged.

"Perhaps one day," Ellie said. She opened the door to leave and carefully made her way down the front steps. Landing on her backside or spraining an ankle, as Muriel had, was the very last thing she needed.

Plumes of smoke pumped from the kitchen chimney at McClure's, and as Ellie neared the porch, she traced delicious scents wafting from Audrey's kitchen. Going to the side door, rather than the front, Ellie kicked as much snow from her boots and hem as possible before bursting into the warm kitchen.

"There you are!" Audrey cried from where she stood at the stove. "I was about to send Caleb to the infirmary. Gracious, did you just crawl out of a snowdrift?"

Ellie sat on the long bench next to the door and started unlacing her boots—but the laces were wet and frozen and impossible to work with. Finally, she gave up and tugged the boots off, tied laces and all. They landed with twin *thunks* on the floor, and her wet stockings left darkened splotches on the wood. A shiver raced up her back.

"You need something hot in your belly, and quick," Audrey said before pulling a mug from a shelf and opening a muslin bag. She scooped in two heaps of black tea leaves and poured boiling water over them to let them steep in the mug.

"Come away from the door, there's a draft." She motherhenned Ellie over toward the stove and peeled off her cold, stiff jacket. Until then, Ellie had forgotten she was still wearing her nightdress. They laughed at how absurd she appeared as Audrey wrapped one of her own shawls around her shoulders.

"What news have you heard?" Ellie asked, as once again she tried to warm up with a cup of something hot in her hands.

Audrey threw her a glance but didn't get out a word before the kitchen door swung open. Maggie entered, her normally wild, red hair tightly braided and twisted atop her head in a neat bun. She was a solemn young woman, but she'd been smiling more lately. Her sister, Fiona, was nearing the end of her first pregnancy and sent letters at least once every week from Grantstown where she lived with her husband. After having spent a number of months estranged because of a disagreement over Fiona's choice of a husband—and her living situation, which was above her husband's saloon, The Silver Strike—the two sisters were finally mending their relationship.

Maggie's cheeks looked especially rosy this morning.

"Have you heard from Fiona?" Ellie asked. She had a midwife in Grantstown, but Ellie was naturally interested in her condition.

Maggie blinked, seeming taken by surprise at the question. "No, doc, why do you ask?"

"Oh, it's just that you looked so happy, I thought you might have had another letter." But then she felt silly for assuming that was the reason why.

Maggie's cheeks reddened even further. "Do I? Look happy, I mean?"

Audrey and Ellie crossed an amused glance.

"Slightly more so than usual, yes," Audrey agreed. She took a pan of biscuits from the oven, the tops perfectly golden. Ellie's stomach crimped with sudden pangs of hunger.

Maggie tucked a loose strand of hair behind her ear and

shrugged. "I can't see why that would be. I was just out shoveling snow on the front porch. Maybe it was the fresh air?"

Ellie sipped her tea, recalling Caleb being on the front porch with the shovel when she'd come toward the boarding house. She hadn't seen Maggie outside, however.

"I'm on my way to the Bookers," Maggie went on, taking a basket from the countertop and laying down a towel inside. "Can I bring some of these buns leftover from last night?"

Audrey kept a large, yellow, metal breadbox painted with bright red poppies on the counter, and its two shelves were always stuffed with baked goods.

"Of course, take them. I need to make room for these biscuits anyway," she answered.

Ellie's appetite waned and regret filled her as Maggie placed four buns into the basket. Mrs. Booker was a miner's wife with two small children who Maggie tutored a few days a week. The boys weren't welcome at the Sage Canyon schoolhouse on account of their skin color—the schoolteacher, Mrs. Newsom, had made it clear only white children were welcome. It infuriated Ellie that someone would bar a child from a schoolroom simply because they were black, but that wasn't why her belly suddenly felt hollow from nausea instead of hunger.

Mrs. Booker had come to the infirmary once, but after the truth of Ellie's scandal in Boston came out, she had made it clear she wouldn't be returning. They'd passed each other on the street many times since, and though Ellie tried to say hello, the woman only hurried along with nothing more than a polite nod. Letting the brushoff go was proving to be a challenge.

Maggie wrapped herself in her green jacket and left the kitchen in a hurry.

"Did that seem a bit strange to you at all?" Audrey asked.

"You mean the fact that she wasn't on the porch shoveling? I saw Caleb out there, not Maggie," Ellie replied. "It's a small lie, but why lie at all?"

Audrey looked thoughtful as she finished setting the biscuits on a tray to cool. "It's probably nothing. She's a good girl, not prone to deviousness. I'm not worried." She raised an eyebrow and grinned. "Yet."

Ellie nearly groaned in delight when Audrey placed a biscuit on a plate and brought it to her. She took the chair across from Ellie.

"You asked what news I've heard," she said as she sat down.

Ellie nodded, her mouth full.

"It's vile, but you're bound to hear it, so it might as well come from me." Audrey leaned forward. "There's a rumor quickly taking hold that there was no break-in, as Nate Walker has claimed."

The much-too-large bite of biscuit slid down her throat too slowly. She took a quick sip of tea and spluttered, "What do you mean?"

"A few people I've spoken to this morning are saying Nate himself shot Frank and is making it look like a break-in."

Ellie coughed on a leftover crumb and took another sip of tea. "That's absurd! Why would Nate shoot Frank now? He and Myra are married, they're having a child. Frank had made his peace with it."

Or so, everyone in Sage Canyon had come to believe. But the odd look on Myra's face came back to Ellie again. She shook her head. "No. I don't believe it. Nate Walker is trying to turn his life around. He wouldn't do this."

He'd seemed genuinely concerned when he'd arrived at the boarding house, too.

Audrey sat back and sighed. "I agree with you. But rumors can be nasty things to stomp out. What did Deputy Munns find?"

Ellie told her about the back door, open to the driving wind and snow, the postmortem, and the removal of the bullet. She also told her Jack would be assisting Munns—in an unofficial capacity, at least.

Audrey blinked, surprised. "Really? I have to say, that makes me feel a little better. Oh, don't get me wrong, I think Charlie Munns is a fine young man, but...if I'm being honest," she lowered her voice, "he doesn't strike me as sheriff material."

Ellie bit her lips against an answering grin. He had certainly appeared squeamish at the sight of the dead body.

"How is Jack?" Audrey asked, and by the curious glint in her eyes, Ellie knew what she was really driving at.

She wilted in her chair. "I just don't think he has the same feelings for me anymore."

One of the qualities Audrey possessed was not saying anything she didn't mean. Usually, Ellie appreciated such straightforward manner—she had learned the importance of honesty, even if it came across as harsh. So, Audrey's reply really shouldn't have hit her as hard as it did.

"I'm sorry, Ellie. I really am. For what it's worth, I think Jack did take a liking to you right away. You're intelligent and beautiful and can most certainly go toe-to-toe with his temper."

"But?" Ellie could hear it coming.

"*But—*" Audrey grimaced "—his wife's death practically destroyed him. I suspect he feels guilty for the feelings he has for you."

Ellie set down her mug. "I suspected the same thing."

Thinking it to herself was one thing; admitting it out loud and having someone she trusted confirm it was quite another.

"He isn't ready yet," she murmured. Audrey reached out and clasped her hands around Ellie's, which were still around the middle of the mug, warming.

"Give him some time."

It was a good piece of advice, though it fell through her like a penny tossed into a deep well.

Thankfully, the clomping of boots came into the kitchen. Ellie knew Caleb's heavy stride by now. For a quiet young man, he was certainly loud in his approach.

"Caleb! Boots!" Audrey cried jumping up from the table at the sight of snow tracked into her kitchen from the entrance hall.

"Sorry," he murmured, eyes cast to the floor. "I forgot. A letter's come for you, Doc Ellie."

She stood up, grateful for a reason to escape into her room. "Thank you, Caleb," she said, taking the letter. Cold radiated off his jacket, his cheeks bright from the cool air and exertion from shoveling.

When Ellie saw the handwriting and the return address on the envelope, she all but forgot where she was and what she was doing. She didn't realize she was standing in one of the wet puddles Caleb had tracked in.

"Ellie?" Audrey's concerned voice filtered in through the sudden pounding of her pulse in her ears. "Is anything wrong?"

Ellie dragged in a breath. "No, of course not. Don't worry, it's just a letter from home." She then raced upstairs toward her room.

It was a letter from home, but it wasn't from her sister or her parents.

Matthew Benton, her ex-fiancé, had written her.

CHAPTER 4

*T*he unopened letter sat on her bed while Ellie changed out of her nightdress and wet stockings and into something more respectable.

The clothes she'd brought with her from Boston had been sensible, like high-necked shirtwaists in cream and yellow and blue, a black gore skirt, a brown tweed pleated skirt, and a deep purple linen skirt with side pleats and abalone buttons. In a moment of weakness, she'd also included an elegant Worth gown. She would likely never have an occasion in which to wear it, but she still indulged in the luxurious sight of the burgundy silk every time she opened the closet door.

What she had not taken into consideration was the severe cold that a Colorado mountain winter would unleash. Thankfully, she'd been able to procure some more under layers for her skirts and a heavy woolen jacket, along with a lovely knit scarf from Katherine and a pair of mittens from the Cameron family. Mrs. Cameron had made them for Ellie as a humble way to thank her for helping save her little girl's leg after a rockfall crushed it. Then, not long after, Ellie had a hand in rescuing their son Ben from West Mountain, where he'd fallen into a crevasse. Although, Nate Walker had been the one to really rescue him.

It wasn't surprising that Nate was suspected in Frank's death —the two men had been at odds because of the way Frank had treated Myra. As Ellie dressed in the brown tweed skirt and cream shirtwaist and pulled on new, dry stockings, she resolved to turn her thoughts away from the confusion surrounding the murder and toward something else just as bewildering.

She eyed the letter on the blanket. The bed was made and the fire stoked. There was nothing else for Ellie to do to procrastinate any longer.

Wrapping a shawl around herself, she snatched the envelope up and perched on the edge of the mattress. It was the first letter she'd received from Matthew. He hadn't even bothered to say goodbye before she departed Boston, and yet, just weeks before, the two of them had been planning to spend the rest of their lives together. As her heart picked up speed and her stomach flipped, she wondered what in the world could have inspired him to write to her now. She also wondered what, exactly, she was feeling. Dread? Excitement? Pure curiosity?

Whatever it was, it certainly wasn't indifference.

Ellie dragged in a bracing breath and read:

Dear Ellie,

I hope this letter finds you well in the mountains of Colorado. I apologize for not writing sooner—I did not wish to make you uneasy with a letter from me when we did not part on the warmest of circumstances. I also did not dare contact your sister or parents right away for your address, especially after a rather frigid encounter with Miss Pearl on Weymouth Avenue in October.

Ellie bit her lips against a smile, imagining how Pearl must have treated him. She had always been her most stalwart defender, and when Matthew called off the engagement after she was banished from the medical community and practically all civil society, Pearl had been livid on Ellie's behalf. Ellie, however, had been resigned—and not truly surprised.

I have, regretfully, let too much time pass before writing to apologize for my actions late last summer. I know how much you appreciate succinct and unflowered language, so I will say it straight out—I was wrong, Ellie. I allowed my reputation within the law firm to guide my decision instead of my heart.

Ellie's breathing turned shallow and slow. The tips of her ears heated. Was this a hallucination? Was she truly sitting here, reading these words from Matthew?

I have missed you, and while I don't expect you to share my feelings, let alone reply to this letter, I do hope you will consider both. I wish you well, Ellie, and a merry Christmas.

My continued affection,

Matthew

With shaking fingers, she lowered the single sheaf of paper to her lap and stared at the inked words. Her eyes jumped from one sentence to another, though not necessarily in order. *My continued affection... I was wrong... apologize for my actions... share my feelings...* Doubt reared its ugly head in the back of her mind, telling her these things couldn't possibly mean Matthew still had feelings for her, that he regretted calling off the wedding. That he wanted her back.

He'd described the way things had ended as not the warmest of circumstances, but Ellie wouldn't have chosen those words. It had been ice-cold. He'd simply ceased to see her, to speak to her. When Matthew had finally arrived at her family's home after weeks of avoiding her, he'd remained standing within the front sitting room entranceway and recited without an ounce of emotion that it would be best if she ceased planning their wedding ceremony. He'd told her to keep the engagement ring he'd presented her with if she wished; it wasn't a family heirloom and as such he wouldn't require its return. He'd then bid her good luck and farewell.

She'd been too broken from the consequences of Todd Andrews's death to argue. Why *should* Matthew marry a woman the whole of Boston considered at best a failed physician, and at worst, a murderer?

But now, with this letter...was he truly regretful of his decision?

And did it matter?

Ellie folded the paper and slid it back into the envelope. Despite the dry, warm clothes and the heat on her cheeks, she shivered. She hadn't a clue how to respond, so she put the letter in her desk drawer where she would leave it until she could form coherent thoughts on the situation.

What *did* it matter, though? Matthew was in Boston. She was here, thousands of miles away, starting over. Not very successfully, perhaps, but she'd still committed to being here, and she'd helped a good number of people so far. The longer she was here, the less she thought about her past, which included Matthew. If she were being honest, he hadn't crossed her mind in days. Maybe weeks.

Ellie quit pacing the rug in her room and went back to the kitchen, resolved to do something more useful than fret over a letter she was starting to wish had been lost on its way west.

THE FOLLOWING MORNING, the Colorado sunshine was steadily melting the snow. By mid-morning, Audrey and Ellie had filled a basket with biscuits and a container of chicken soup and set out for Eberly's store. The snow on the street had been cleared away by a horse-drawn plow the afternoon before. The plow, an arrow-shaped pair of heavy wooden boards, had sliced through the snow and shoved it aside in great heaps. There was quite a banking in front of Eberly's for Ellie and Audrey to climb over in order to get inside.

As Ellie entered, she was struck by the memory of what she'd seen the morning before. Frank's dead body on the floor, a shivering and shocked Myra at his side. Tension coiled in her shoulders as she thought about what Audrey had heard, the rumors about Nate Walker being the murderer. Myra sat behind the counter, on a tall stool, a piece of knitting in her lap. Dark circles puffed the skin beneath her eyes.

"Myra, you should be upstairs, in bed," Audrey gently admonished—something Ellie knew she herself would never have gotten away with. She was far too new in town to be giving orders to mourning women, but Audrey was a mother hen, and everyone knew it. More so, they expected it.

Myra got up from the stool and set her knitting on the counter. The wool yarn was a lovely shade of cream white, the stitches small and formed into a delicate lacy pattern. No doubt she was making something for her unborn child.

"I had a hard enough time sleeping last night," she said, leaning heavily on the counter as she came around to greet us.

"Where is Nate?" Ellie asked.

The edges of Myra's lips tugged down into a frown. "With Deputy Munns."

Silence blanketed the room. Ellie's pulse picked up speed. "Oh no, Myra...has he been arrested?"

Myra's pale skin suddenly flushed bright, and her eyes turned hostile. "Arrested? Why would you assume such a thing?"

Heat speared Ellie's chest as flames of regret consumed her. She parted her lips but was unable to speak. Audrey said the rumors about Nate's involvement were rampant, but they clearly hadn't reached Myra yet. She longed to snatch back the words and shove them down her throat.

Audrey's eyes widened and she, too, parted her lips at the blunder.

"It's just a rumor I heard, and I shouldn't have paid it any mind," Ellie said quickly.

"No. You shouldn't have," Myra bit out.

Somehow, even Ellie's eyes felt hot with embarrassment. She set the tin of soup on the counter and backed up. "I really should be getting to the infirmary. I'll see you at McClure's later, Audrey." She bobbed her head and forced a smile, but Myra's stony expression didn't soften in the least.

Ellie left the shop as swiftly as she could. The cool mountain air alleviated only some of the livid blush that had seared her cheeks and neck. Her mother had always admonished her for being awkward and socially inept, and truly, Ellie knew she lacked the social graces other women of her acquaintance in Boston possessed. Pearl, for instance. Even though she was a handful of years younger, she always knew what charming thing to say. All Ellie could think of as she made her way across the street toward the infirmary was how grateful she was her mother had not witnessed that clumsy blunder.

As expected, there were no prospective patients lined up on the porch, but Ellie entered the infirmary anyway, if only to slam the door behind her and exhale with a small growl. Why must she always say the wrong thing at the wrong time? Ellie closed her eyes and leaned against the door, the cold window glass pressing against her back. It seemed as if this town would forever make her second-guess everything about herself.

An image of Jack immediately formed behind her closed eyelids. After the few kisses they'd shared, Ellie had thought things would develop further between them. Instead, the reverse had happened. Matthew came to mind, and how their relationship had fallen apart, too. She'd read his letter again the night before and had laid out a sheet of paper to begin a response. The page remained blank this morning on her desk.

The glass at her back rattled as a fist knocked upon the door. Ellie jumped forward, startled, her heart skipping. A woman and a young girl stood on the porch. Ellie shouldn't have felt so eager

—no one visited a doctor when they were feeling well. Taking a deep breath, she opened the door.

"Good after—"

The woman rushed inside, ushering the little girl forward. "Lulu has a terrible cough and a fever."

Ellie blinked and then closed the door behind the pair. The mother kept her arm braced around the young girl's shoulders, who certainly did have the glazy-eyed, pink-cheeked look of an elevated temperature.

"Why don't you have a seat up on the table, Lulu," Ellie suggested. She went out back to pump a bowl of water, washed her hands quickly, and tied on a pinafore. The little girl, who looked to be five or six, was in the middle of a coughing fit when Ellie approached with the thermometer.

"I'm Doc Ellie," she told Lulu, and then looked to the girl's mother. "I don't believe we've met yet."

"Mrs. Dorothy Winthrop." Her expression twisted with worry. "Dottie," she added quickly.

Dottie looked as if she wanted to say more but pinned her lips together and focused on Lulu. Once the coughing subsided, Ellie took her temperature, and sure enough, the mercury rose a degree above one hundred.

"When did she become feverish?" she asked, gently feeling the girl's glands on the side of her neck. They were warm and swollen.

"Last night," Dottie answered. "And she's been coughing for a few days."

Dottie wrung her fingers together; they were red and chapped, and Ellie noted that the woman's skirt hem had a few char holes. From standing close to a fire or stove at home, most likely.

Ellie set down the thermometer and took a small peppermint stick from the glass jar on her desk. Lulu's eyes had lifted to the jar a few times already.

"Here, suck on this for a minute while I talk to your mother." The little girl's hot fingertips brushed Ellie's hand as she quickly accepted the candy.

Pulling Dottie toward the back of the room, she lowered her voice. "Is there something more you'd like to tell me? You look extremely worried over a small fever and cough."

The two cold symptoms were so common, Ellie wouldn't be able to prescribe more than rest, hot fluids, and perhaps some honey to coat her throat. She could always ask Tamora for a poultice, she supposed.

Dottie checked over her shoulder before speaking in a whisper. "Last winter…there was an outbreak of diphtheria."

Ellie gathered a breath. She had heard of the outbreak. The pharmacist in Grantstown, a rather unpleasant man named Doctor Goodwin, had mentioned it when Ellie first visited his shop. He'd refused to sell her medicine via post, not trusting that she was in fact licensed and capable of dispensing it, and it had taken a trip to his drug store in person to convince him.

"I've been told," she murmured, a chest-constricting premonition rising. A moment later, Dottie confirmed it.

"My littlest…he was just a year old…well, he…" The poor mother couldn't finish her sentence. There was no need. The tears filling her eyes and the quiver of her lips and chin were enough. Ellie placed a hand on her shoulder.

"I'm so sorry, Mrs. Winthrop."

There was never anything adequate to say when speaking to a parent about the death of their child. Ellie always searched for something, some phrase that might give comfort or peace. But she could never conjure anything beyond heartfelt condolences.

"Lulu had it too, but she recovered, and I just worry that perhaps it's back. Her throat…it looks speckled to me."

Ellie returned to Lulu on the table and the crisp scent of peppermint. The little girl paused her licking long enough to tip back her head and open her mouth wide. With relief, Ellie noted red tonsils but none of the whitish-gray mucous that coated the back of person's throat when diphtheria was present.

Dottie exhaled audibly and a smile wobbled onto her lips. "If you're sure?" she asked as she helped Lulu down from the table.

"Yes. Do come back or fetch me at McClure's if she appears worse, or if you see anything forming."

Ellie prayed it was just a cold, as she suspected. A diphtheria outbreak, in a remote town such as this, would be devastating. It was highly contagious, and the antitoxin now being used to treat the ill would most certainly not be available.

"Thank you, doctor," Dottie said as Ellie gave her a second peppermint stick for the walk home, and Dottie placed the quarter fee onto the desk.

After they'd left, Ellie picked up the round of silver and slipped it into her skirt pocket with a sigh. Well, she certainly wasn't going to get rich at this pace. A small grin touched her lips, and she laughed. She hadn't gone into the profession to become rich anyhow. Her family had always been wealthy—in fact most physicians were. Few who weren't could afford the cost and luxury of attending university. No, she'd become a doctor to help people when they were at their most desperate. Treating sick children was especially rewarding.

Ellie chewed on her lower lip as she removed her pinafore and washed her hands again. Treating children could also be devastating. Todd Andrews still haunted her, the image of his peachy cheeks and fuzzy upper lip as he slept in his medical bed never far away. It was as if nothing more than a thin, fluttering film of muslin on a washing line stood between her and him; if the muslin caught the wind just right, it would blow aside and there he'd be. The gnawing ache of guilt in her chest and stomach had not lessened in the least, and she wondered if it would always be that way. If she'd simply have to learn to live with it.

To distract herself, Ellie went over the postmortem notes she'd taken on Frank Eberly, and after an hour or so of waiting around, wondering if another surprise patient would show up at the infirmary door, Ellie put on her coat, folded the postmortem into her doctor's bag, and left for the sheriff's office. Deputy Munns was bound to be finished with Nate Walker by now, and indeed as she ascended the steps to the office and opened the door, she found him seated with his boot heels on top of his desk —or rather, Sheriff Payton's desk—reading what appeared to be a telegram.

His eyes landed on Ellie and he fumbled to sit up and lower his feet to the floor. "Doc Lennox," he said, belatedly remembering to stand up to greet her. Charlie Munns, while a bit of an oaf, was a good man and gentlemanly. Ellie liked him. Most of the men she'd met in Sage Canyon—and women too—had a hard edge, formed by necessity. Life was not easy or gracious out here. But Deputy Munns lacked that hard edge. He reminded Ellie of some of the men she'd known in Boston, like Matthew for instance.

Ellie reached into her doctor's bag and took out the postmortem. "I thought you'd like to have this."

He took the paper and gave it a cursory glance. Lines notched between his eyebrows.

"It's the postmortem," she provided at his look of confusion. "Stating the specifics of how Mr. Eberly died."

He lowered the paper and set it on his desk next to the telegram he'd been reading. "Man was shot," the deputy said. "Simple as that."

She gritted her molars and suppressed a groan. "Yes, well, this is an official statement, which will be needed during a court trial."

"Unless we make an arrest, there won't be one."

Ellie skirted around the rumor about Nate Walker. "Are there no suspects?"

Deputy Munns sighed heavily. "Could be. I shouldn't discuss it with you, what with you being a citizen and all."

Ellie crossed her arms. "Please tell me you don't suspect Mr. Walker."

His eyes leaped to hers, and he practically jumped in surprise. She suppressed a grin. The man did not possess the slightest bit of guile.

"Where'd you hear that?" he asked.

"This is a very small town, deputy," she replied, not wanting to mention Audrey's name. "Did you find any boot prints behind the shop?"

It had been less than half an hour between the murder and Ellie's arrival at Eberly's. The snow had been coming down in drifts but perhaps a print or two had managed to remain.

He shook his head. "Nothing. The snow's up to my knees behind the shop."

"What about the bullet I pulled from Mr. Eberly?"

"Granger's looking into it," he replied. Ellie nodded. She felt somewhat guilty; Deputy Munns was just so affable. Certainly, if Sheriff Payton were present, he wouldn't have answered her questions.

The deputy picked up the telegram again and his lips pulled into a grimace.

"Bad news?" she pressed.

He regarded her a moment, as if questioning whether or not he should answer. Then, he sighed and tossed the telegram onto his desk again.

"It's Marshal Bevins," he replied. "He doesn't want Jack helping the investigation in any way, shape, or form."

She nodded. "I've heard the two of them aren't on good terms."

That left Munns on his own, and it certainly looked as if he was lamenting that fact. Perhaps he just wasn't the sort of man to take charge of a situation.

"What does Sheriff Payton have to say about it?" she asked.

Deputy Munns seemed to wilt as he scratched under the brim

of his hat. "I sent a wire to Denver and asked it be directed to Payton's relations there. Haven't heard back yet."

Reaching the sheriff might take some time, especially in a city the size of Denver. Until then, Munns—not Marshal Bevins—was the one handling the investigation.

"Well," Ellie continued, "considering Sheriff Payton is away, and *you* are the one making the decisions in his absence, I'm sure no one would fault you for engaging a second opinion on matters."

Deputy Munns frowned but seemed to be pondering her meaning. The marshal wasn't in Sage Canyon. There was no reason he needed to know Jack was helping.

"If you need anything, I'll be at the infirmary or McClure's," she said.

As she left the sheriff's office and walked back up Main Street, Ellie's feet slowed at the sight of a familiar horse tied to the post outside the boarding house. Tamora's dapple gray was covered in a red and black blanket, a worn black saddle, and leather saddle bags stitched with beads. The animal swished its tail side to side, and mud speckled its back legs. She hadn't seen the Arapaho midwife for a few weeks and wondered why she'd come to Audrey's today.

Inside the boarding horse and tavern, frantic voices sounded from the kitchen. Once there, Ellie found Tamora standing at the stove, holding her hands just above the flat iron top to warm them. Ellie's stomach cinched at Audrey's expression of concern.

"What's wrong?" she asked.

Audrey's cheeks paled. "Another man has been shot."

CHAPTER 5

*E*llie's doctor's bag suddenly weighed more than its usual eight pounds.

"He stumbled to my door early this morning," Tamora said, turning away from the stove. Her long black hair, streaked with silver, cascaded around her broad shoulders in loose waves. Tamora was an imposing woman in stature but also in presence. She easily commanded any room she walked into.

"Is he still alive?" Ellie asked.

"He was when I left my place," Tamora answered with a dubious shrug. "But he's in rough shape. I figured I'd fetch you to see what more could be done, if anything."

Two shootings in the same number of days. Ellie frowned and nodded. "Let's go."

"I'll send Caleb to Jack's, and I'll go to Deputy Munns," Audrey said. "They'll meet you there."

Tamora and Ellie left McClure's, and after awkwardly mounting the dapple gray, behind Tamora, the two of them rode down Main Street.

"Do you know who it is?" Ellie asked, her doctor's bag

awkwardly slung over one elbow, her arms gripping Tamora's waist.

"Hank Jerrick," she answered. The name didn't immediately ring familiar, and Ellie let out a sigh of relief. It was selfish, but she was glad the victim wasn't someone else she knew.

"You know this man?" she asked next, as they trotted past the line of identical, whitewashed, stick-built homes where many miners and their families lived.

"He was a member of the Hodge gang. Like Nate Walker, he cut loose after the shootout here in town."

Ellie gathered a breath and held it, surprised, and more than a little concerned. Jack had struggled with his vendetta against the Hodge gang. She wondered how he'd react to hearing one of them had come back to town—even one currently suffering from a gunshot wound.

They passed the mining entrance, which was a mire of snow and mud and rubble. Tamora's horse snorted and struggled to trudge through it. The hardy girl pushed onward, though, and they made their way onto the main path up West Mountain, toward Tamora's cabin in the woods.

"Where is the bullet wound?" Ellie asked, eager to begin planning her treatment, if only in her mind.

"An inch or two below the left clavicle," Tamora answered. Too close to the heart, Ellie thought, her hope flagging. Tamora went on to explain the bullet was lodged and a lung sounded punctured.

"Normally, I wouldn't leave a person in such dire condition," she added. "But considering he was likely to die anyway, I figured it was worth the try."

"It doesn't sound promising," Ellie admitted. When Jack had been shot, the bullet had gone through and no organs had been damaged. Pure luck, really. Or perhaps Nate Walker, whom Jack had startled at Eberly's store, hadn't wanted to kill him. It was possible he'd tried to aim for a survivable spot.

With the thought of Nate Walker, Ellie frowned. An ex-Hodge gang member had been shot, and yesterday, the new father-in-law of an ex-Hodge gang member had also been shot. The connecting threads concerned her.

Up the mountain's path, a mess of horse hooves and boot prints marred the thick blanket of snow. Tamora slowed the horse.

"Is something wrong?" Ellie asked.

Tamora eyed the prints in the snow. "Could be."

With swift and sure movement, she reached into the saddle scabbard for her rifle. She continued on as Ellie's pulse began to knock against her neck. The hoof prints and boot prints were new, Ellie assumed, and with mounting dread, she saw they turned toward Tamora's cabin.

"Stay here," the midwife ordered, dismounting with lithe movements that defied her age. Ellie fumbled with her doctor's bag and dismounted as well but without Tamora's sure-footedness.

Tamora raised her rifle and went around the back of the cabin rather than onto the front porch. Ellie waited, her breathing notched, feeling uncertain and ineffective. She edged a little closer to the cabin, inspecting the prints in the snow. It was a chaotic mix of boots and hooves. Whoever had been here, they looked to have left.

The front door opened from the inside, and Tamora appeared, her rifle lowered. "You can come in."

Ellie knew something was wrong as soon as she entered the small, dark log cabin. Melted snow puddled the floor from where boots had tracked it inside, and on the cot set up before the hearth, a man lay unnaturally still.

Ellie rounded the kitchen table and approached the cot, hardly breathing. A blanket lay half off his legs and drooped toward the floor, as if he'd struggled to sit up and push it off. Blood stained his shirt in a wide, dark splotch, but it was the neat hole in the man's forehead that turned Ellie's stomach. She covered her mouth with her gloved hand and backed up, her heel catching on a braided rug.

"Looks like someone came to finish him off," Tamora said, standing watch in the open doorway, rifle still in hand.

Ellie composed herself, letting the shock of the situation fade as her mind turned to the wounds the man had sustained. She set down her bag and approached the body. Tamora had placed a poultice wrap over the first wound, below the clavicle. This, Ellie left alone. Blood, still relatively wet, speckled the man's lips and chin. He'd coughed on blood as the liquid had inundated his respiratory system. A bullet to the brain would not have caused this, so she assumed his punctured lung had filled with blood. A pulmonary hemorrhage would have been deadly on its own. Whoever tracked him here could have simply waited for him to expire.

Unless his assailant wanted to be sure Hank Jerrick couldn't say anything to anyone.

Ellie shivered as a gust of cold air entered the cabin from the open door. She hoped the riders wouldn't be coming back, but it seemed Tamora wasn't taking any chances. Knowing that Jack and Deputy Munns were being alerted, and that they might already be on their way, gave her some comfort.

She inspected the wound under the poultice wrap, but truly, there was nothing to be done. Ellie stood and joined Tamora at the door.

"By the mess of prints in the snow, it appears it was more than one person," she murmured. Tamora agreed with single nod. Her dark eyes watched the trees surrounding the cabin until finally, she stepped back.

"We're safe," she declared, and then turned to enter the kitchen. She laid her rifle on the table. "Tea?"

Ellie wrapped her arms around herself, the cold air still gusting inside. She shut the door and accepted the midwife's offer. It was indeed surreal to sit at the pockmarked wooden table and sip on peppermint tea while a dead body lay not ten feet away. Neither Ellie nor Tamora said much of anything as they waited. When the jangle of tack and a man's voice sounded from outside the cabin, Ellie jumped to her feet.

"It's just Jack," Tamora said. She slowly stood up and went to the door. As soon as she opened it, Jack was there, rushing into the cramped kitchen.

He stopped short at the sight of Ellie. "Are you okay?" he asked, breathless.

Flummoxed, she nodded. "I'm fine."

His eyes swept the small space and landed on the cot. After a long exhale, he said, "I saw tracks in the snow coming up from my place. Looks like a posse fled in that direction from here."

"They came while I was in town getting the doc," Tamora explained.

Jack took off his Stetson and gestured to the body. "I'm guessing he didn't arrive with a bullet in the head."

"The first shot was to the upper sternum," Ellie said. "Tamora thought I might be of some help and came to get me."

Jack tossed his hat onto the table, the brim sliding against Ellie's mug of tea. He raked his fingers through his flop of tousled hair. "That's Hank Jerrick. He has ties with the Hodge gang."

"Tamora told me," Ellie said. "Do you think the men who did this are connected to the Hodge gang too?"

He clenched his jaw and, like Tamora had, peered out the small window into the trees. "Whoever they were, they're dangerous men. If they'd still been here when you two arrived…" He turned a tight circle, his hand again raking through his hair.

Jack looked at Ellie, concern brimming in those grassy green irises of his. They were a bright, lively color, and many times, she'd felt trapped in them.

"Doc would have been fine," Tamora said after a momentary silence. "I had my rifle."

Was that what truly worried him? Her safety? Ellie wanted to reach for his arm and reassure him, but he broke his trouble gaze and moved to the body's side. He hitched his hands onto his hips.

"Coming here to finish him off was risky," he said, mostly to himself.

"Perhaps the men knew Tamora would bring people up here and they didn't want to chance Mr. Jerrick saying anything revealing?" Ellie suggested.

"You think this is connected to what happened to Frank?" Tamora asked.

Ellie noticed how calm the midwife seemed to be about everything. While shivers raced up and down Ellie's arms and legs, Tamora remained unaffected. She wondered how she could be taking it all in stride.

"The timing sure is peculiar," Jack muttered, crouching next to Jerrick. "Where's his piece?"

Tamora opened a drawer in her kitchen hutch and removed a pistol. "I took it soon as he showed up this morning."

"You hear the first gunshot?" Jack asked next.

Ellie quickly determined Tamora must have—Jerrick would have needed to be close by to make it to her cabin with a chest wound.

"Thought it was a limb breaking under the weight of the snow and ice," she answered. "Sounded like it came from up the trail."

Jack reached into the man's pockets, turning up nothing more than a few dollars and coins, a box of matches, a handkerchief, and some folded papers. He was sorting through his findings when another horse and rider turned toward the cabin. Deputy Munns dismounted and came up the porch at a less eager pace than Jack had shown.

"Hank Jerrick doesn't have any family or friends around here," the deputy said as soon as he'd been filled in on everything. He looked a little queasy and tried to stay a good step from the body. "What's he doing in Sage Canyon now?"

"Did he say anything when he arrived?" Ellie asked Tamora. She had gone into another room and brought out a sheet of brown canvas. She laid it on the floor, next to the cot.

"Just that 'they' had shot him. Then he collapsed on my floor." Tamora removed the blanket that Jerrick had been partially covered with and with Jack's assistance, transferred the body onto the canvas.

He and the deputy carried Jerrick's wrapped figure to Munns's horse and draped him over, in front of the saddle.

"I'm going to have to wire the marshal," Munns said as he mounted the horse. "Sounds to me as if we've got a posse up here connected to the old Hodge boys."

Jack nodded. "I'll have another talk with Walker."

"Try not to let Bevins get wind of it," Munns said, his eyes skipping to Ellie's briefly. It seemed he'd taken her advice about keeping Jack involved, even if it was against the marshal's wishes.

Ellie's worry grew as Munns tipped his hat and turned from the cabin. Two men had been killed in two days, and it all felt too ominous to be unrelated. She returned to the cabin for her doctor's bag and when emerging onto the porch again, heard Jack asking Tamora, "You'll be all right up here?"

She scowled at him, then laughed. "Get on out of here, Granger," she said, shooing him away with a wave of her hands.

Jack flashed her a bashful grin, then faced Ellie as she stepped off the porch. He nudged up the brim of his hat. "I'll bring you back to McClure's. If you don't mind riding together?"

He eyed her skirt. Although he was most likely only assessing whether or not she should ride astride or side-saddle, her pulse skipped. Her long and voluminous skirt would allow her to ride astride without showing too much ankle and petticoat. Ellie forced the girlish anticipation of a ride with Jack from her mind and took his extended hand.

Jack settled behind her in the saddle, and with his arms closing around her to take the reins, he eased his white-and-brown painted mare, Fern, from Tamora's cabin. Ellie kept her spine rigid as they followed in Deputy Munn's wake.

"You know, we're going to have to get you your own horse," Jack said, his chest vibrating. He leaned forward and added, voice hushed, "Not that I mind sharing a saddle with you."

Ellie twisted around at his teasing tone and warmed at his playful grin. For the first time in weeks, being with Jack gave her a bubbly sensation rather than one of confusion. A tremble of awareness ran through her as Jack readjusted his hold on Fern's reins.

She tried to focus on the problem at hand, rather than his scent of wood smoke and the peppery blue sagebrush that lingered on his coat. The snow now covered all the wild brush out near his ranch, so the scent must have been from before the weather turned.

"What is your opinion of this Jerrick fellow?" she asked.

"Pure scum. He wasn't like Walker, who just followed the Hodge boys like a trained pup. Jerrick and Jeb Hodge were close."

"He wasn't arrested and convicted as Hodge was?"

A number of Hodge gang members were jailed, including Jeb Hodge. But the gang's leader, Jeb's older brother, Chet, had evaded capture.

"No." Jack slowed Fern as she descended the track, the snow cover torn apart by a couple passes of horse and rider traffic. "I'm surprised he dared come back around here. Must be something that attracted him."

Jack's arms tightened around Ellie as Fern picked up speed down a little knoll, her long neck bobbing with each stride, her honey-blonde mane ruffling in the wind. His hold on the reins nearly closed Ellie into an embrace—though of course that was silly. He meant nothing by it. Still, a fleeting image of Jack wrapping his arms around her and pulling her close, lowering his lips to hers, ran through her mind.

"Could be that Jerrick tried to pay Walker a visit the other night and got Frank instead," Jack mused. Ellie cleared her mind and focused on what he was saying. "Jerrick could have shot Frank and ran off."

"Then who shot Jerrick? And twice, for that matter." Ellie twisted as far as she could in the saddle. "You don't think Mr. Walker?"

Jack's unconvinced gaze slid against hers. He then looked to the path ahead again. "I'm starting to think Walker's got something to do with this, whether he knows it or not."

Ellie didn't quite know what he meant by that, but before she could ask, they were within sight of the Canyon Creek Company silver mine. A crowd of miners, in their soot-streaked coveralls, stood together looking after Deputy Munns, farther ahead on the road.

"Granger." Mr. Roberts, the owner of the Canyon Creek Company, came to the front of the crowd. He wasn't wearing coveralls but a casual suit and sensible, tall boots. Ellie clenched her jaw.

The last she'd heard, Mr. Roberts had planned to bring in his own company physician for his miners and their families, which would only deplete Ellie's possible number of patients. But over the last few months, she hadn't heard anything more on the matter.

"Roberts," Jack greeted. It wasn't overly warm. Ellie knew the two weren't necessarily friends, though she'd learned little more about why.

"Mind telling us what's going on? Charlie Munns just rode past here with a body draped over his horse. Wouldn't part with so much as a word."

Fern slowed as Jack tugged the reins. "The deputy has his reasons to stay tightlipped for the moment."

"That's two men dead this week," Mr. Roberts went on, undeterred. "My men have families to think of."

"If there's trouble brewing, we don't want to leave our wives and children alone," another man said. He was the only black man in the grouping of whites. Though Ellie had met a few other black folks in Sage Canyon, Mary had said they were the only black family attached to the mine. This, she presumed, must be Mr. Booker.

Jack held up a hand. "There's no reason to think your families are unsafe. I'll talk to Munns."

Mr. Roberts crossed his arms and eyed Ellie. "Ma'am," he said, acknowledging her, then turned and headed back toward the operation. His workers slowly followed.

Jack nickered to Fern, and they began moving again.

"*Ma'am*," he teased, leaning a little closer to Ellie's ear as he had before.

She laughed. "I prefer Doctor."

"I'm aware of that," he replied with a short laugh. In all honesty, Ellie loved that he called her Doc more than he did Ellie.

"Mr. Roberts is aware of it too, no doubt," she said. "It's his subtle way of letting me know what he really thinks of me."

"I wouldn't take his opinion to heart."

"Oh, I don't," she said. "I've made many men uncomfortable and upset just by doing something they believed only *they* could do. Mr. Roberts is at least tactful in his disdain."

Fern loped toward Main Street. Ellie wondered if Jack was slowing their pace intentionally.

"Have you heard from your family back in Boston lately?" he asked.

Ellie stiffened in the saddle. She didn't know why his question surprised her. Perhaps because he'd never asked after them before.

"Is everything all right?" he asked when she didn't reply right away.

"Oh, yes, sorry," she said quickly. "I had a letter from my sister the other day. They're getting ready for Christmas."

She wouldn't say anything about the unexpected letter from

Matthew. No one in Sage Canyon knew she'd been engaged, not even Audrey. She'd never had the occasion to bring him up in conversation, or a reason to explain that she'd been engaged. That he'd called off the wedding was also a source of humiliation. Why mention it if she didn't absolutely have to?

"I suppose it'll be hard to be away from home for the holidays," Jack said.

"It will be. My mother loves Christmas. You should see the way she decorates the rooms in our house." Ellie rolled her eyes and shook her head. "You'd think she expected Saint Nick himself to attend the annual Christmas gala."

Jack adjusted the reins in his gloved hands. "Gala? Sounds a bit fancier than the dance the church here hosts every year."

Ellie's grin slipped. She also hadn't delved into how well off and connected her family was.

"My father is a senator," she admitted, oddly nervous. She checked over her shoulder to see Jack's reaction. His golden brows furrowed.

"A politician? Why'd you never say?"

Ellie shrugged. "I suppose it never crossed my mind to."

That wasn't entirely true. Jack tucked his chin, holding her stare as if to tell her he knew as much.

She sighed. "Oh, all right. I didn't say anything because...well, I wanted people in this town to look at me as one of them. If they knew I was a rich senator's daughter from back east, it would be just one more thing to set me apart. I want to do this on my own, without his influence, without his money. And I have."

Jack led Fern to the hitching post out front of McClure's. He dismounted, then helped her to the ground. She clutched her doctor's bag, her face hot from her confession. Jack hadn't made his reply yet. She worried his opinion of her had changed now that he knew.

"I used my own savings to outfit the infirmary. It's one of the reasons I didn't look into the shopfront you showed me a few months ago. I couldn't stomach wiring my father for—"

Jack cupped her cheek, silencing her. His smooth leather glove cooled her flushed skin.

His eyes danced with amusement for a moment, then turned serious. "Doc, you don't need to prove anything to me. Where you come from, who you come from, none of that matters." His thumb swished over the apple of her cheek, but then hastily, he lowered his hand and took a step back. "I'm just grateful you're in Sage Canyon."

Her lips went slack, her shoulders dropping all tension. "You are?"

Again, amusement lit his eyes. "You sound surprised."

"It's just been a little while since you…well…" How could she say it without sounding brazen? Perhaps she couldn't. "Kissed me," she whispered, another zing of heat licking up her neck.

Jack sighed, and his smile slipped away. She regretted being so bold now, but at the same time, knew it had needed saying, consequences be damned.

"Funny thing is, I imagine kissing you about a dozen times a day."

Ellie stared up at him in shock. He wasn't trying to be humorous. His gaze was still steady and clear. Serious.

"Why don't you then?" she asked, surprising herself.

"Well, I hardly think barging into McClure's and the infirmary to log in twelve kisses a day is exactly suitable," he replied with a renewed spark of humor. "There might even need to be a kiss or two at Toft's or the post office to get to a dozen, which would only cause gossip."

Ellie smacked him on the arm but was grateful he'd cracked a joke; the embarrassing flush broiling her cheeks, neck, and ear tips began to recede. He laughed, rubbing his arm in mock hurt. His grin, however, faded too soon.

"Truth is," he said, and she knew he was not joking anymore.

"The feelings I have for you are mixed up with a whole lot of guilt. I know it doesn't make sense. Sarah's gone, and she isn't coming back, but I can't help feel...*wrong* about wanting you, doc."

The honesty made her breathless. He *wanted* her? Heavens, no man had ever expressed such bold desire for her before. She bit her bottom lip in contemplation.

"I suspected you felt guilty. I understand. Really, I do," she added when he looked at her in doubt, as if he wanted her to argue with him. Perhaps it would make things easier for him if they could fight about it, and he could stalk away.

"You still love her," Ellie said softly. Nothing more than a prick of jealousy edged its way under her skin. The poor woman had been killed in a shootout, and she'd only been in town on an errand. To buy cloth for a shirt she intended to sew for Jack, too. She'd been ripped away from a loving husband.

"I always will," he admitted, again looking guilty.

"As you should." Ellie took his hand in hers and squeezed it. "Jack, I don't want you to feel guilty about caring for someone other than Sarah. Perhaps it's best if we just remain friends for now."

She hated saying the words. They tasted like poison on her tongue. What she wanted, desperately, was for Jack to shake his head and tell her no, that's not what he wanted. But as he tensed his jaw and looked down at their joined hands, pausing for too long a moment, Ellie knew she wasn't going to get her wish. He nodded sadly.

"I should've said something to you before now, doc. Friends might be best."

She drew in a breath and forced a tight grin, as if she'd expected this response. As if it was what she'd hoped for.

"Good. Friends then." She squeezed his hand again and let go. "I'm glad we have that behind us. Now, I should get inside and let Audrey know what's happened. She must be worried sick."

Ellie abruptly turned and took the front steps at a pace that belied what she was truly feeling inside: the crush of her heart and the threat of tears. Jack didn't follow her in. Ellie closed the door, and instead of going to the kitchen, she took the stairs to her room, where she could sob in privacy.

CHAPTER 6

"*I* can't believe you talked me into this," Ellie muttered. She stood behind a long table inside the community church. Pies, cookies, and cakes stretched from one end of the table to the other.

Audrey stood beside her, smiling at every person who strolled by. "It's a church raffle, not a hanging," she replied softly while also nodding hello to Mrs. Kemp, a well-liked seamstress in town.

The annual holiday bake sale and raffle kicked off Christmas in Sage Canyon, Audrey explained earlier in the week when she'd recruited Ellie to help. At the time, she'd agreed readily.

"Then why do I feel as though I'm walking to the gallows?" she now hissed.

Nearly every lady had glared at her as they approached the table, which was filled with delicious looking and smelling items. An old pickle jar was quickly filling up with slips of paper, though a few ladies had refused to drop in their tickets simply because Ellie was the one holding the jar.

"Never mind them," Audrey said, then peered over at her. "I'm surprised—I didn't take you for the sort to quail under a little pressure."

The jab was intended to work her up into froth, though in a good-natured way. Audrey knew full well that Ellie would not cower from a few upturned noses and huffs of indignation.

After Muriel Carson and her husband, the mayor, had all too eagerly revealed the truth about Todd Andrews's death back in September, there had been a devoted number of women and men who refused to give Ellie a second chance.

"I'm not quailing," she replied and then forced eye contact with Mr. Mattson, the banker, as he approached the table.

As one of the mayor's friends, Mr. Mattson had been cool toward Ellie when she first entered the Grantstown Extension Savings and Loan, and while he hadn't refused her service, he certainly hadn't been welcoming.

"Mr. Mattson, good afternoon," Ellie said brightly. Perhaps a little too brightly—the man jumped back a step, brows rising.

"Uh, good afternoon, Miss Lennox." His attention shifted back to the sweets on the table.

"Doctor Lennox is accepting the raffle tickets," Audrey said, emphasizing *doctor*. Ellie had given up trying to convince some townsfolk to address her properly—Mr. Mattson included.

He was a bachelor in his mid-forties with a receding hairline, but he had a rather handsome and dignified face—straight nose, strong chin, clear blue eyes. If he wasn't such a stick-in-the-mud, Ellie would have suggested the equally handsome Audrey take a shine to him. Then again, she'd only been a widow for a year. Her husband had been one of the handful of victims last winter's diphtheria outbreak had claimed. Audrey never spoke of it. There must have still been too much pain attached to the topic.

Mr. Mattson coughed. "Yes, well, erm…I must say this pie looks absolutely delicious." He took out one of the tickets he'd purchased at the door and slipped it into the jar. "I hope you nab my ticket when it comes time to draw for it."

He spoke solely to Audrey, and from the attention he paid her, it was obvious he had at least taken a shine to her.

After he'd moved along to the table of needlepoint pieces up for raffle, Ellie nudged her with her elbow. "He isn't too curmudgeonly, is he?"

Audrey snorted, which was so unladylike for her that Ellie startled and laughed.

"*Much* too curmudgeonly," Audrey whispered. "He's far too different from my George."

Ellie jumped on the opportunity. "How so?"

Audrey sighed, her deep brown eyes staring out at the busy church. Pews had been removed to accommodate the foot traffic, but it was as if Audrey was seeing something else, looking back in time, searching her memories.

"George smiled a lot. He loved the sound of laughter and would try his hardest to get every person he met to bellow loudly at least once," she said, laughing herself, then shaking her head. "Do you know he even got Muriel Carson to laugh once?"

Ellie parted her lips in shock. "No!"

"Yes! He was walking toward her on Main Street when he devised his plan. He tipped his hat to her, pretended to stumble over something, and fell face first into a mud puddle! Oh, that man! He was covered in muck, but his sacrifice was worth it. Muriel let out a laugh that sounded just like the braying of a mule." Audrey covered her mouth to smother more laughter.

Ellie did the same, unable to believe it. Muriel Carson braying like a mule was perhaps one of the most ludicrous things imaginable. The stern-lipped, sour-faced woman was far too haughty for anything like that.

"George must have been very proud of himself."

"We laughed for days and days," Audrey said, the apples of her cheeks rosy, the fine lines around her eyes showing. She truly was a striking woman, and Ellie wondered why no gentlemen from Sage Canyon had yet to approach her. Or perhaps they had, and none had measured up to her first husband. Perhaps true love was all Audrey was willing to settle for and hers had already come and gone.

Ellie sighed out a last bit of laughter. "I would have loved to have met him."

"He would have adored you," she said, but then the happiness fled from her smile. Now, it was simply wistful.

A few ladies came to the table, gawking at the chocolate cake. As soon as they dropped in their tickets, Audrey resumed speaking.

"George worked for the mining company when we first came to Sage Canyon. He lasted nearly ten years before the dust in the mines started to really bother him—he was terribly sick with pneumonia when he was a child, and it damaged his lungs."

"He quit the mines?" Ellie asked.

"He did, and that's when we started the hotel and tavern." The memory brightened her expression again. "We poured ourselves into it and loved it so much that George wished he'd quit the mines years earlier."

It was evident Audrey loved her hotel and tavern, and Ellie wished she could have met George, too. Before either of them could say anything more, however, a familiar face appeared before their table.

"Mr. Yeaton," Ellie greeted the postmaster. He smiled and extended not a raffle ticket, but a Western Union telegram.

"This came for you, Miss Lennox. I figured I'd bring it by since I was on my way to the church. Have you had the chance to taste my wife's preserves?" he asked, gesturing toward a table across the church floor where dozens of glass jars were on display.

"I can't say as I have," Ellie replied, amused by the question and also curious as to who had sent her a telegram.

"You really must, then, they are summer-in-a-jar," he said

with a look of pure bliss. With that, he made a short bow, and cut his way across the floor toward Mrs. Yeaton's table.

"Summer-in-a-jar," Audrey whispered. "My, my, that man is certainly devoted to his wife's...fruits."

Ellie gasped and stared at her, while Audrey clapped a hand over her mouth and giggled like a young girl. Ellie couldn't help but do the same as she opened the telegram's envelope. When she slipped out the paper, her smile foundered.

"Bad news?" Audrey asked.

"I'm not sure." Ellie re-read the telegram.

> *Need to meet. Bring your sheriff. Imp. Hodge details.*
> *-R.R.*

"R.R.," Audrey repeated after Ellie read the telegram aloud. "Your reporter friend, Miss Ruthers?"

Ellie had met Rachel Ruthers on the train into Grantstown and the two had quickly become friends. She was from Chicago and was a thoroughly forward-thinking female reporter seeking adventure in the Wild West, a place where she could really make her mark. Ellie supposed they had gotten along so well because they were both intrepid, with jobs that were typically held by men in society. But it had been Rachel's open and welcoming personality that Ellie had truly taken a liking to.

"Yes. I wonder what she could mean by important Hodge details," Ellie murmured, folding the telegram and putting it into her skirt pocket.

"She must have heard about the two killings here," Audrey suggested.

It had been three days since Hank Jerrick had been shot at Tamora's. It was more than enough time for word to have spread to Grantstown, which was just a few miles down the tracks. Deputy Munns had been trying to downplay the worry that some

Hodge gang members might be back in the area, though unsuccessfully—the whole town was whispering about the possibilities.

"Sheriff Payton's not back," Audrey continued. "You won't be able to bring him to meet with Miss Ruthers."

Ellie sighed and her chest grew tight. "She doesn't mean Sheriff Payton."

The few times Ellie and Rachel had met over the last few months, she'd called Jack "your sheriff," aware of Ellie's feelings for him. At first, Ellie had claimed Jack wasn't her *anything* but slowly, she'd started to hope… Though now, she'd have to somehow tell Rachel that Jack wished to be just friends.

Audrey arched one brow. "I see. Why would she want to meet with Jack too?"

"She must know Jack's history with the Hodge gang," Ellie said. It was exactly why she *didn't* want to bring Jack with her to Grantstown. How tempting would it be for him to fall back into an obsessive frame of mind?

A crowd of townsfolk approached the table and for many minutes, the only talk was of the raffle, the sweets, and the other offerings around the room. Ellie sneaked a look at her pocket watch, a dainty gold fob her sister had given her ages ago. She was starting to feel restless. Should she heed Rachel's request and ask Jack to go with her? Or perhaps she could go on her own. But what if it truly was important that he be there?

Her mind was still tangled in knots when, across the table, a throat cleared. Ellie blinked, looked up from the jar of raffle tickets in her hands, and met the dark-eyed stare of none other than Doctor Goodwin, the brooding pharmacist from Grantstown.

Ellie snapped to attention. "Doctor Goodwin? What are you doing here?"

Audrey coughed lightly, and Ellie realized how utterly rude her greeting had been. She set down the jar and tried again. "I mean to say hello, how are you?"

Doctor Goodwin shook his head. "Charmed, as usual, Doctor Lennox." His deep voice cut through the din of chatter in the room.

He was in his early thirties, perhaps, with dark eyes and hair, a perpetual grimace, and pair of wire-rimmed glasses that gave him a studious appearance.

"I apologize, you just surprised me. I hadn't expected to see you in Sage Canyon."

He turned his attention to the cakes and pies, though Ellie couldn't imagine him actually craving anything on the table. He didn't seem the type to have a sweet tooth.

"I'm just here on business," he said.

Ellie clasped her hands behind her back. Doctor Goodwin had said that to her before, the last time she'd crossed paths with him in Sage Canyon in late October. She'd been walking along Main Street and had turned her gaze from the glorious autumn colors on the mountainside in time to see him coming up the street from the depot. At that meeting, he'd said he was here on business, too, and had artfully dodged Ellie's question about what sort. Twice more she'd seen him in town, though she hadn't been close enough for so much as a greeting those times. She still longed to know what business he spoke of but couldn't bring herself to pry—at least not with Audrey standing right next to her.

"Well, if you need a place to stay for the night, there are rooms available at McClure's," Audrey said. Ellie peered at her, hearing a touch of curiosity on her tone.

"Thank you, but I'll be taking the three o'clock train back to Grantstown."

"The raffle drawing is at two," Ellie said. "Perhaps you'll win something to take home with you."

Doctor Goodwin raised his eyes to hers and smirked. "I'd be eating pie for a week."

"Or cake."

His smirk became a full smile. The sight of it took Ellie by surprise. She nearly teased him about it, but she wasn't quick enough. He nodded his head in parting and started away, toward the neighboring table.

"He is certainly serious," Audrey whispered as he continued to amble around the room and give the offerings critical inspection.

Their initial introduction had been less than amiable back in September, but he'd proven to be dependable when it came to shipping her medicines. It made her think of something.

"I'll be right back," she said to Audrey and then moved out from behind the table. "Doctor Goodwin," she called. He turned on his heel, his brow furrowed in concern.

"Doctor Lennox?"

"I wondered if you might have received any of the diphtheria antitoxin we spoke of a few months ago?"

Ellie had checked in on Mrs. Winthrop the day before, and her daughter's fever had broken, thank goodness. A slight cough lingered, but there still hadn't been any of the mucus build-up on the back of Lulu's throat that would indicate diphtheria. Dottie had been so relieved that tears had slipped down her cheeks before she could blink them away.

If possible, Doctor Goodwin's frown deepened. "Is something wrong?"

"No, not that I am aware of, but there was a mother whose little girl was sick, and apparently this mother's other child passed away during last winter's outbreak. It got me thinking that perhaps having some of the antitoxin on hand would be a good idea."

He let out a long-suffering sigh. "Unquestionably. However, it seems antitoxin has a difficult time making it past Denver."

Ellie shook her head. "I don't understand."

The crowd around Mrs. Yeaton's preserves table grew thick, and Doctor Goodwin and Ellie agreed with a shared glance to move toward the church doors. Once they'd descended the front steps into the dreary afternoon weather, he explained.

"The antitoxin is difficult to create, so there is a limited supply of it, and it's usually designated to the larger cities, where outbreaks have the likelihood of being much deadlier."

"I see," she murmured. Sage Canyon was but an afterthought compared to a city like Denver. Still, it wasn't right to withhold a medicine from a place simply because fewer people might die here rather than in a larger city. "Could you keep trying?"

Doctor Goodwin's expression was one of doubt, but he didn't argue. "Persistence comes naturally to you, doesn't it?"

"It does." She then bit back a grin and added, "To my mother's discontent."

It won another smirk from the pharmacist, and Ellie had the fleeting thought that it would be nice to see more of them. "I'll send another request to the lab in Philadelphia."

She thanked him and then, after a somewhat awkward pause, he nodded tightly and walked off, toward the depot. Back in the church, Ellie found Audrey at the sweets table, all of her creations looking like something straight out of one of Boston's finest bakeries.

"You should sell your pies and cakes at the mercantile," she suggested, stepping back behind the table.

"I could speak to Katherine about it." Then, with a sly grin, added, "And perhaps she could tell us more about Doctor Goodwin's visits."

Ellie picked up the jar of raffle tickets and frowned. "What do you mean?"

"It's where he goes whenever he's in Sage Canyon."

"Toft's?"

His business was at the *mercantile*? Audrey nodded, but then grimaced.

"I shouldn't gossip. But I admit, I'm curious. It seems once a month, Doctor Goodwin arrives, visits the mercantile for an hour or so, then leaves for Grantstown again."

Ellie hugged the large pickle jar closer to her as she took in this new information. Could he be visiting with Katherine? She was quite pretty, and they were about the same age. But why would Doctor Goodwin say he was here on business if it was a social call? And one that only happened once a month, at that.

The final hour of the church raffle seemed to drag on for a decade, but at last all the winning tickets were drawn, the sweets disappeared into the eager hands of the winners, and Audrey and Ellie strolled back to McClure's arm-in-arm. Caleb had helped them that morning, transporting all the items to the church, but he wasn't needed now. So, when Ellie and Audrey entered the boarding house through the kitchen door, they weren't surprised to see Caleb standing with Maggie by the countertop. What was quite astonishing, however, was the way they leaped a good arm's length apart with twin blushes staining their cheeks.

Ellie and Audrey came to an abrupt stop just inside the doorway. The kitchen ballooned with uncomfortable silence. The chapped appearance of Caleb's and Maggie's lips revealed exactly what they had been doing. Ellie hinged shut her dropped jaw.

"Caleb? Maggie?" Audrey said hesitantly as she closed the door.

"Audrey, I...well, I was just about to...go set the tables in the dining room," Maggie said, then turned and rushed from the kitchen.

Caleb was left standing there, his face lowered, eyes pinned to the floor. Ellie cleared her throat. "I should, ah, check in at the infirmary." She quickly backtracked out, onto the porch. She covered her grin with her hand as she left Audrey to deal with the discovery of her son's romance.

It had been obvious to Ellie for quite a while that Caleb adored Maggie. Ever since she had recovered from a dangerous fever that nearly took her life a few months ago, he would leap to her side whenever she needed help, even if it was just the usual task of carrying towels to the cabinet or bringing in firewood. He would look at her with admiration whenever she spoke, too. But Ellie hadn't thought Maggie returned those feelings.

Then again, her blush earlier that week after she'd claimed to have been shoveling the porch made a little more sense. Perhaps she'd simply been watching Caleb shovel from the front hall windows? With a light bounce in her step as she made her way to the infirmary, Ellie giggled again at the embarrassment on both of their faces at almost being caught locked in a kiss. She didn't think Audrey would be angry at the two taking an interest in one another—at least she hoped not. Ellie was certain it was all innocent enough.

At the turn for the infirmary, Ellie paused, her eyes on the far end of Main Street, where the town's cluster of stick-built storefronts and buildings ended, and small farms and homesteads began. The two mountains created a valley here in town, but as the foothills of the mountains ended, the valley parted and became flat ranch land.

Ellie patted her skirt pocket, where she'd stowed Rachel's telegram. *Bring your sheriff with you.* He wasn't sheriff, and he wasn't her anything any longer, but ignoring Rachel's request felt like the wrong thing to do—even if it was a mighty temptation. It would be so much simpler to catch the first train to Grantstown tomorrow morning all by herself, but as Ellie had learned by trial and error many times before, the easiest route was not always the right route.

Jack's ranch was a good twenty-minute walk from town, and it was barely three o'clock. She could make it there and back before sundown, she was certain. With feet heavy as lead, she continued past Green Street, and headed in his direction.

CHAPTER 7

*T*he train rumbled over the narrow tracks leading toward Grantstown. The morning had sprung with a clear blue sky, and Ellie had walked toward the depot to meet Jack, as they'd planned the afternoon before, with more eagerness than she'd expected. The few trips she had taken into the larger town just two miles down the winding tracks had given Ellie room to breathe. Sage Canyon was so small, so clustered, and while Grantstown was certainly nothing at all like Boston, it at least had multiple blocks of streets and a large number of businesses.

Being out of Sage Canyon, where half of the small population still looked at her with disdain, would indeed be a treat. However, being alone on the train with Jack and just one other soul—a clerk for the mining company who sat several rows ahead of them—was nearly indescribable a feeling. Ellie's pulse still skipped whenever she saw Jack, and yet his confession that he wasn't sure if he was ready for a romance with her tamed that skipping pulse with a firm hand.

Friends. They were going to be friends. Ellie *did* want that. She'd rather be friends with Jack than nothing at all. And who knew? Maybe this feeling of thrill whenever she caught sight of him would fade with time. She certainly hoped so.

Ellie watched the landscape through the windows as they approached town, her hands folded in her lap. She'd worn a slightly more fashionable dress for the occasion. It was made of maroon tweed and was paired with a short black jacket and black kid gloves. Her teardrop hat was also black. Now that she really thought of her attire, she wondered if she didn't look a little too somber.

"What are you frowning at?" Jack leaned forward in his seat to peer out the window. "I'm not entirely sure those trees deserve such a scowl."

Ellie looked away from the window and met Jack's wry grin. "I was thinking about my dress."

She instantly regretted blurting it out the moment he turned his eyes to her figure. "What about it?"

She shook her head. "It's nothing, really. I suppose I've just grown used to wearing simpler garments in Sage Canyon."

They were far more comfortable; Ellie found it hard to believe that she'd had a whole closet filled with stuffy and elaborate dresses back in Boston. Even the ones she'd considered efficient and packed for her trip west had turned out to be too fancy for her new life.

"Like nightdresses?" he said. Ellie's mouth popped open, and a burst of laughter emerged, unbidden. Until right then she'd entirely forgotten that she'd attended to Frank Eberly in her nightdress.

"I'll thank you for not bringing that up again!"

Jack sat back in his seat. "Okay, okay, but I can't promise not to think of it every now and then."

A fierce heat licked her skin at the notion of Jack thinking of her in her nightdress. She straightened in her cushioned seat as the train whistle blew. The outskirts of Grantstown were in view now, a scattered collection of homes and barns and paddocks. Quickly, the city proper appeared, with its clapboard sided buildings and homes, brick and mortar shopfronts, lampposts, and to Ellie's unexpected delight, red ribbons and garland strung from many of them.

"I nearly forgot it was Christmastime," Jack said as they stepped from the train and found the depot dressed for the upcoming holiday.

"My mother loves Christmas," Ellie said as they crossed the tracks and made their way toward a main road. "But I've already told you that, haven't I?"

"What about you?" he asked.

"Me?" Ellie slowed. No one had ever asked her if she liked Christmas before. It had always been her mother's holiday...as if it belonged to her and her alone. On Christmas morning, the attention was always on what gift her mother might fawn over the most. Ellie and Pearl would compete each year to think of the best one to give her.

"I think I do love it," she said as they stepped up onto the sidewalk.

"I didn't think it would be such a hard question," he laughed.

"Sorry, it's a long story, but in short, Christmas revolves around my mother, not me or my sister."

Now that she heard herself saying it, it did sound a little strange. The holiday was supposed to be a magical time for children, and while her mother had made the house feel magical, Ellie still had never felt it was for her or Pearl.

"It's silly, I suppose. Just a holiday, like any other."

Jack walked alongside her, matching her pace toward the *Grantstown Current*, the paper for which Rachel Ruthers wrote.

"Audrey puts on a nice dinner," he said softly. "She's invited me the last few years."

"Does she?" A mutinous spark of excitement lit under her skin. The thought of Jack arriving at McClure's on Christmas, of sharing a dinner with him, was enough to scatter her resolve not to react to him anymore.

"You won't mind spending the evening with me, I hope," he said, his shoulder coming close to hers and brushing against it lightly.

"Not at all," she replied.

Jack came to a stop. His eyes lifted, and Ellie spent a shameless moment drinking him in—the straight lines of his nose, his defined jaw; his clear eyes and a mouth that smirked more than anything else. Two fine parentheses creased his cheeks from the expression, too, but they only made him appear more handsome.

"This it?" he asked. Ellie snapped to attention and realized what he was looking up at: the sign on the front of a building. It was the *Current*.

Ellie had sent a telegram to Rachel the evening before, announcing that she and Jack would be on the first train the following morning. They entered the front door, into an immediate cacophony of clacking typewriter keys, ringing bells, raised voices, shuffling feet and papers, and somewhere in the din, the incessant chirping of a bird. It was all coming from up the stairs, set to their immediate right.

Ellie climbed with Jack on her heels.

"You should know, I really don't like reporters," Jack said.

"Oh, I'm quite aware," she replied. The afternoon before, when she'd arrived at his ranch and told him about Rachel's request, he'd glowered something fierce. She hadn't shown him the telegram, not wanting him to see how Rachel referred to him as "your sheriff."

"Any particular reason why?" she asked.

"They made me look like an unhinged madman hunting down my wife's killers," he said, and like always, the mention of his wife left behind the barest prick of envy. It was absurd, considering the poor woman was dead.

"You must know by now that all reporters want is to captivate their readers," she replied. "I'm not saying it's right, but it's part of their business."

He grimaced, and as they reached the top steps, Ellie reached for his arm, her fingers touching his elbow. "Trust me, I know just how painful reading a vicious article in the paper about yourself can be. I had my fill back in Boston."

Wretched headlines like *Female Doctor Kills Child* and *Incompetent Woman Doctor Murders Boy* worked their way into her heart and soul until she'd started to feel a tremor of dread every day upon waking.

Jack captured her hand and came to a standstill at the top of the steps. "I'd thought of that," he said. "For some reason, I can't see you caring about what anyone has to say about you."

She shook her head, and a sad huff of laughter gusted over her lips. "I wish I didn't."

For a short while, Ellie had refused to get out of bed, too afraid of what the papers would print about her. Too afraid to even leave her house.

Jack gave her hand a small tug, and she caught her breath as it brought her closer to his chest. He cocked his head, meeting her eyes. "Nothing they say means anything. You're a damn good doc, don't ever let anyone make you second guess that."

If she could have wrapped her arms around him, she would have. However, Ellie settled for a friendly squeeze of his hand. "Thank you. And whatever the papers printed about you, it's not who you are."

He held her gaze. "Who am I then?"

To her embarrassment, the unexpected question rendered her speechless. She blinked; her lips parted, but she remained silent. Jack's serious expression lightened, and he grinned, but a shadow of disappointment lingered before Ellie heard her name being shouted.

"Ellie! Over here!"

Rachel waved her arm from the middle of the open, second

floor office space. About a dozen others were seated behind desks or crossing the room with purpose.

Taking a shaky breath, Ellie started toward her friend, who was—as usual—wearing what appeared to be a skirt, but upon closer inspection, were a pair of black tweed gauchos. Rachel had claimed to love trousers so much that she planned to never put on another skirt again. Ellie had to admit, she was curious about trousers, but figured it wasn't worth alienating even more people in Sage Canyon.

"You made it, I'm so glad," Rachel said, dropping into her chair as soon as she'd given Ellie and Jack each a pert handshake.

As there was nowhere for Ellie or Jack to sit, they stayed standing in front of her desk. A momentary awkward silence enveloped them. Jack put an end to it.

"You said you know something about the Hodge gang."

Rachel leaned forward and clasped her hands together on top of her ink-blotter. "I just might."

"Might?"

Ellie flinched at Jack's annoyed tone.

"Miss Ruthers, are you saying you called us out here on a *might*?"

Ellie understood his exasperation but held up her hand to allay him. "I'm sure it's more than speculation?" She drove a hard look at Rachel, beseeching her to come through with something more than what she'd offered so far.

"Depends on what you're willing to do for the information," Rachel replied. Ellie's chest locked up with irritation.

"Rachel, what is this about?" Leaving Sage Canyon for what would amount to a full day meant she might not be available if someone became ill or if there was an emergency. Granted, there hadn't been one in quite some time, but on the off chance, it worried her.

Rachel lowered her voice. "I've got a contact. He used to ride with Hodge. He'd like to speak to Mr. Granger, but wants immunity from the law first."

Beside her, Ellie felt Jack go rigid. "Who is it?"

Rachel didn't blink. "Can't say. Won't say, until you give him what he wants."

"Jack's not sheriff," Ellie said.

Rachel shrugged and sat back, as if bored. "I hear he may as well be since Payton's missing."

Ellie gaped at her. "He's hardly missing!"

"I've got someone who says Munns couldn't get a telegram through to him."

"The sheriff is in Denver," Jack said. "Munns is fully capable—"

"Munns is a joke," she cut in.

"That's unkind, Rachel," Ellie said.

Her friend managed to look at least a little remorseful. "My contact won't talk to Munns, period." She shifted her gaze to Jack, who sighed.

"I have no authority to grant him immunity. You know that."

"That could change," Rachel replied. She leaned forward again. "If you're the one who brings in Chet Hodge, you could get your badge back."

The bait, so cleverly dangled, had the desired effect. Ellie's stomach dropped at the intense focus that flooded Jack's expression. She set her doctor's bag on top of Rachel's desk with a *thunk*.

"Your contact wants to give up the leader of the Hodge gang?" For some reason, it didn't seem reasonable. Or believable.

"He isn't square with what happened to Hank Jerrick," Rachel explained.

Jack braced his hands on the edge of her desk. "Chet's the one who dealt with Jerrick?"

The small hairs on Ellie's arms stood on end at the dangerous tone of his voice. The sly humor that usually danced in his eyes was gone, replaced by pure wrath. There was no question that he believed Chet Hodge was the one at fault for not just Jerrick's murder, but his wife's.

"Maybe. Maybe not." Rachel stood up, perhaps not liking Jack staring down at her. She braced her hands against the desk, just as Jack was. "You want to talk to him, you'll have to offer something worth his time."

Ellie felt entirely out of the conversation. Rachel had wanted Jack here to bargain with, and Ellie had been her conduit. She gritted her teeth against the sour taste it left in her mouth.

"And what do you get out of this, Rachel?" she asked.

Finally, her tenacious friend spared her a look. "A helluva good story, that's what. An exclusive glance inside the Hodge gang."

Jack scowled, as if the idea itself sickened him. "Why would you want to give scum like them attention?"

Rachel swung out her arms. "Why wouldn't I, if it sells a record number of papers? Evil sells, Mr. Granger. People love to read all about what scares them."

Ellie shifted her footing and rubbed her temple, wishing she'd followed her first instinct and not brought Jack with her. She felt reeled in, like a fish.

"They killed my wife," he reminded her.

Rachel straightened her back, effectively chastised. Guilt pulled some of the eagerness from her dark brown eyes.

"I know. And I'm sorry you've suffered such a loss, I really am. It's why I thought you'd be willing to do this. Chet Hodge needs to be behind bars, and my contact can help you put him there."

Ellie couldn't argue with that last part, at least. Still, she also couldn't shake the feeling that Rachel was manipulating Jack to reach her own desired goal. Ellie's instinct was to shield him.

She turned to Jack. "We know that Hodge is here, and that he's behind Hank Jerrick's killing. He's probably behind Frank Eberly's too. Maybe you don't need to speak to this contact."

Jack dropped his angry glare to the desk, avoiding Ellie's eyes. "If there's one thing Chet's good at, it's hiding. I couldn't track him down before, and I won't be able to now."

"Not without a trustworthy source," Rachel tacked on, smelling victory.

"I won't trust a damn thing that comes out of that man's mouth," Jack said. He rubbed his forehead, as if exasperated. "But I'll listen to what he has to say."

Ellie's heart sank, though she wasn't surprised.

"What's your offer?" Rachel asked.

"If his information leads to Hodge's arrest, I'll let Marshal Bevins know he cooperated. But if I were you, Miss Ruthers, I'd strongly suggest to him that he ride on out of here sooner rather than later. And stay gone."

She nodded and didn't bother trying to mask her victorious grin. "Meet me at the Silver Strike in an hour."

Rachel grabbed her long leather coat from a hat stand behind her desk and dashed off, leaving Ellie and Jack in a dazed state.

"I don't like this," Ellie said as she took her doctor's bag and started for the stairs.

"You're not the only one," he replied.

They left the building and once they reached the sidewalk, Ellie drew in breaths of clear morning air, untainted by ink and cigarette smoke.

"What if this is a way for the Hodge gang to get you alone? This meeting might just be a lure of some sort."

Jack considered it for a few moments, but then shook his head. "They know where I live, doc. If they wanted me dead, they could've cornered me at the ranch."

The rationalization only alleviated her worry so much. Maybe this contact really did want to turn Chet Hodge in. She walked alongside Jack with no direction or destination in mind. They had an hour, it seemed.

"I guess I'll have to pay Bevins a visit," Jack said, sounding less than thrilled at the prospect. "Get a feel for where he stands on offering an informant immunity. His office has a telephone, last I knew, too. If Munns can't get a wire through to Payton, I could see if his relations are on the Bell exchange."

Ellie's father had a telephone in his office at home, and she'd heard him shouting into the receiver a number of times. Ellie, however, had never had the occasion to place a call herself. There were no telephone lines in Sage Canyon, though the idea that here in Grantstown, she might be able to place a call home and hear her father's voice over the telephone cable gave her an odd mix of temptation and trepidation. She didn't know what she would say to him. He and her mother had only written once, and the brief letter had been cool. If only she could place a call directly to Pearl.

"I could meet you at the Silver Strike," she said, letting go of the idea of a telephone call home. "I'd like to check in on Fiona and see how she's getting along."

Jack took her arm, his fingers sliding around her elbow as they quit walking. Why did she feel as if he was going to argue?

"The Silver Strike's a rough place," he said.

"I've been there before," she countered.

"Doc," he started, his hand on her arm still firm. He struggled with what to say next, and Ellie waited, anticipating something irritating and protective. It wasn't that she disliked his protective side—she just appreciated his confidence in her more.

To her surprise, he at last said, "Just be careful. I don't like how close Hodge is. If this informant is at the Strike—"

Ellie covered Jack's hand with her own. "I'll be fine. Trust me."

He let out a sigh and with a quirk of his lips, said, "I do. It's everyone else I don't trust."

He pulled away after another moment and, tugging the brim of his hat, walked off in the opposite direction. Ellie adjusted her doctor's bag in her hands and started for the Silver Strike. It was located just across the tracks at the depot, so she at least knew she wouldn't get lost trying to find it. Fiona would most likely be there, and considering it was just shy of noon, the place wasn't likely to be busy.

As soon as she reached the saloon, the dark windows and calm exterior relaxed her. The first time she'd come here with Rachel, it had been night, and the place had been packed. She preferred it this way instead. The front steps rattled, and when she opened the front door, there wasn't but one lone patron seated at the bar. Behind the bar, stood Billy Walker, Fiona's husband. He recognized Ellie and gave her a cautious, if suspicious nod.

"Doc," he said. "Is my wife expecting you?"

"No, but I was in town and I thought I'd—"

Behind Ellie, someone descended the staircase taking fast, heavy steps. She turned and stared in shock as Doctor Goodwin reached the final stair. He slowed, his passive expression instantly transforming into something guarded.

"Doctor Lennox? What in hell are you doing here?"

CHAPTER 8

*I*t took a moment for Ellie to comprehend Doctor Goodwin's presence. When she did, a rush of heat lapped her neck and flooded her cheeks.

"I…I'm here to see a patient," she said, wishing the floor would yawn wide and swallow her up, whole.

Ellie wasn't so naïve to not know the sort of transactions that went on upstairs. She never would have imagined Doctor Goodwin would be emerging from such a place.

"As was I," he quickly said, gesturing toward the second level as he came off the last step. "It's a, uh, delicate situation."

Ellie spied the leather bag in his hand—a smaller version of her own medical bag.

"How is she?" Billy asked, addressing Doctor Goodwin from behind the bar. The pharmacist shifted his attention to Fiona's husband.

"Better. Resting. She shouldn't see anyone for a few days."

Ellie peered at him, catching on. While the rush of embarrassment eased, her indignation only escalated. "Are you practicing *medicine*, Doctor Goodwin?"

"I'm *dispensing* medicine."

"On the orders of a physician?" she pressed.

He straightened his black cross-over necktie and grimaced at her. "It's a simple enough diagnosis and treatment. I'm more than qualified."

Considering Doctor Goodwin's patient, Ellie could take an educated guess about what he'd been dealing with. A venereal infection, most likely.

He lowered his voice and stepped closer. "What are you doing here anyhow?"

"She should see a physician," Ellie persisted.

"Good luck finding one in Grantstown that will risk his reputation to treat her." He took a breath to clear the anger that had fueled his remark and lowered his voice. "What are you doing in a place like this, Doctor Lennox?"

She clenched her jaw. "Not worrying about my reputation, that much I can tell you."

He raised both brows, crinkling his forehead. "I think I already knew that."

"Very funny. I'm here on business."

He frowned, as if recognizing his own words being thrown back at him. "Is that right?"

"Yes." She had nothing to hide from him, unlike his concealed reasons for coming to Sage Canyon once a month. "My friend's sister is expecting. I've come to check in on her."

The tension in his shoulders relaxed somewhat as Billy joined them at the bottom of the steps.

"My wife's feeling poorly this morning, doc. I'm glad you've stopped in."

A stroke of concern pushed her irritation with the pharmacist to the back of her mind. "Take me to her, and I'll see if there's anything I can do."

"This way," Billy said, and then started for the door next to the bar. Ellie eyed Doctor Goodwin.

"Good day," she said primly, still feeling awkward about their run-in.

He set his bag on a table. "I'll wait here, if you don't mind."

Ellie's feet tripped to a stop. "Whatever for?"

He looked as though he'd swallowed a particularly bitter dose of cough syrup. Softly, he said, "I'm not leaving you alone in a saloon, Doctor Lennox."

Her lips parted on a gust of surprise. A laugh escaped next. "That's totally unnecessary, I assure you. Mrs. Walker is an acquaintance."

He responded by pulling out a chair at the table, sitting down, and hooking one ankle over his opposite knee. The mule-headed man! Well, she wasn't going to waste time arguing with him, not when Fiona might be in need of a doctor. She rolled her eyes toward the ceiling and turned to follow Billy into the back rooms of the Silver Strike, determined to focus on Fiona and not the exasperating man who had gotten it into his mind that because she was a woman, she required safe handling and protection.

"Men," she grumbled under her breath. Billy turned his ear to her.

"Say something?"

"Not a thing," she replied brightly, forcing a grin. He knocked on a door and slipped inside; a moment later, after a brief, muffled exchange of voices, he opened the door fully and allowed Ellie in.

Fiona was sitting up in bed, propped by some pillows. Her long, fiery hair was in a braid, draped over her shoulder, and she was still wearing a dressing gown.

"Doc Ellie, I wasn't expecting you," she said, her voice somewhat breathless. She rested a hand atop the shelf of her protruding stomach.

"I hope this isn't a bad time?" Ellie asked.

The room was bright and warm, a small stove in the center of the room crackling. The barroom smelled of ale and cigarette smoke, but in here, rosewater and clean laundry prevailed.

"I'm not busy," she replied with a self-deprecating wave of one hand over her current position.

She was only weeks away from giving birth, Ellie knew. Frustration and impatience were understandable emotions. But there was something else in Fiona's eyes. Exhaustion, perhaps. Her coloring, usually pink and healthy, had paled a little.

Ellie took a chair and brought it next to the bed. "Billy says you're feeling poorly today."

Fiona shot her husband, still lurking in the doorway, a displeased look. "You shouldn't fret so. The doctor has more important things to do than check in on me. I'm big as a house and tired as a newborn kitten, though I'm told that's normal."

Ellie unclasped her bag and took out her most used instrument: her stethoscope.

"It is normal," she said, slipping the ear tubes around her neck. "And it's no trouble at all. I'm actually meeting Mr. Granger here soon, so you're giving me something to do while I wait."

"Listen to the doc," Billy said. And then to Ellie, added, "And don't let my hellcat of a wife run you out before you're good and certain she and the babe are well."

He winked at Fiona, who waved her hand at him and told him to shoo. Ellie bit back a grin as she pressed the steel drum to Fiona's chest and had a listen. Her heartbeat was slow, but steady. Then, Ellie gently pressed the drum to her lower abdomen to try and hear the baby's heartbeat. Fiona's stomach moved as the baby wriggled, but after a quiet stretch of about a minute, the faint, quick *woosh-woosh* of a fetal heartbeat came through the earpieces.

"It's a strong heartbeat," Ellie confirmed. Fiona beamed at her.

"Can I listen?"

Ellie passed her the earpieces and waited silently until Fiona's eyes widened at the sound of her baby's heart.

"That's amazing, doc," she sighed, her eyes filling with tears.

Ellie smiled at her awed expression and packed away the stethoscope. "I think you're doing as well as can be expected at this point. Have you seen your physician lately?"

Fiona's bright grin dimmed. "Midwife. Mrs. Bletchley."

Of course. Doctor Goodwin's comment about no doctor sullying their reputation to treat patients at place such as the Silver Strike hadn't been an exaggeration or excuse.

"Well, I'm not far if you need me," Ellie said. Though, in a true emergency it wouldn't be a viable option. Like Tamora, Mrs. Bletchley had certainly delivered countless babies in her years. It was nothing to worry over.

A knot worked its way into Ellie's stomach as she closed her bag and stood up, though it didn't have anything to do with Fiona or her baby's impending arrival. Out in the barroom, Doctor Goodwin still sat, waiting for her. She paused at the door. "Fiona, do you know Doctor Goodwin, the pharmacist?"

She pushed a loose strand of hair behind her ear, and a genuine grin formed. "Oh yes, of course. He gives the ladies their medicine if they need it."

"He comes here often then?"

"When he's needed." She shrugged. "It's true that Billy and I disagree about the upstairs girls, but if they weren't renting the rooms above the Strike, they'd be renting elsewhere. At least Doctor Goodwin does what he can for them."

Ellie nodded, trying to understand what it must be like to have no other option than to barter one's body. She'd been lucky in many ways. The next time Ellie started to feel sorry for herself for one reason or another, she'd have to remind herself of that.

"He's a good man, Doctor Goodwin," Fiona added.

Ellie said her goodbyes and left her to rest. A strange irritation crept under her skin as she walked back toward the barroom. The warm praise for Doctor Goodwin shouldn't have bothered her so much. It wasn't that she'd *wanted* Fiona to complain about him but learning the sour-faced pharmacist had an altruistic habit of helping those in need had distorted Ellie's view of him. If anything, he became even more mystifying.

As she reentered the barroom, Doctor Goodwin got to his feet. She met his eyes briefly as Billy approached her.

"How is she?" Billy asked.

"She just needs rest and patience." Ellie paused to think for a moment, considering what Audrey might suggest. "And perhaps a little chocolate cake."

Billy chuckled and scratched the back of his head. "Thanks, doc, I'll get right on that."

Doctor Goodwin stepped forward. "Chocolate?"

"I find it cures many things," she replied. "You didn't need to wait, you know. I'm meeting people here soon."

A handful of patrons had entered the saloon while she'd been with Fiona. The men turned from the bar and watched her with curiosity.

"I'll stay until they arrive." He kicked out the chair and sat again.

"It's not necessary."

"Stop arguing."

Ellie drew in a breath and sat down in another chair at the small table. It was on the very tip of her tongue to tell him that he was being utterly absurd when she recalled Fiona's high praise of him.

She bit her tongue and let the urge fade. Skeptical of her sudden silence, Doctor Goodwin peered sideways at her, but said nothing.

"What did you give your upstairs patient, silver nitrate?" Ellie asked after a stretch of uncertain silence. "Not mercury, I hope."

Many doctors still prescribed mercury injections for venereal diseases, despite the mounting evidence that it poisoned the body more than it helped.

He sat back in his chair, frowning. "Mercury? I'm not a

barbarian. And silver nitrate's fallen out of favor. Colloidal silver is the most effective."

"Not bismuth or sulphur?"

He shrugged. "If that's all that's available."

But it seemed as though he made sure to have the better medicine on hand. Again, an unsettling irritation pricked at her. "I'm sorry," she said quickly. Best to get it out. "For thinking the worst of you when I saw you come down those stairs."

Surprise and a bit of amusement inched across his lips.

"Don't laugh at me," she said, regretting she'd apologized at all.

"I'm not."

She shifted in her seat. "Yes, you are."

"I'm only wondering how sheltered from the world you've been if you think the worst about men who visit places like this."

Ellie lost her breath and whatever else she had planned to say. "I haven't been sheltered."

"Your father is a senator, wealthy enough to put you through medical college and keep you from the more unsavory aspects of the world."

"How did you...?" She stopped. Of course. His university friend. A fellow pharmacist in Boston had alerted Doctor Goodwin about the Todd Andrews case and had likely told him everything he knew about the Lennoxes.

Ellie stood up. "I won't apologize for my upbringing, and I wish you wouldn't use it against me."

"Where are you going?"

"To another table." She turned her back and took the chair at the first one she could find behind her.

It was silly, really, and she knew it. She felt even more a fool when Doctor Goodwin's tall figure appeared in her side vision. He dragged out the chair next to her, the feet screeching across the wood floor, and lowered himself into it.

"You won't catch me criticizing anyone for how they were

raised," he said, more gently than before. "I'm just saying that maybe you shouldn't think the worst of people who you don't yet understand."

She flicked him a glance, reluctant to admit that he might have a point. It was so much easier to just be angry with him.

However, she finally relented. "I'll keep it in mind."

Before he could make another comment, the door to the Silver Strike bashed open. Ellie startled as Rachel bounded into the saloon toward her.

"There you are, thank heaven!"

Dread spilled through Ellie as she stood up. "What's happened?"

"Come with me, quick. My guy's been hurt."

Ellie clutched her doctor's bag and went to the door. Doctor Goodwin followed on her heels. "Your contact?" Ellie asked.

As Rachel fled the saloon, Ellie's heart raced at the idea of another man having been shot down like Frank Eberly and Hank Jerrick. But her mind stayed focused, prepared. Panic wasn't an option.

"Where is he?" she asked as Rachel crossed the train tracks and headed for the depot. "How is he injured?"

"He's down the tracks a little. I didn't want to move him," Rachel called back as she ran. "He's been dragged."

Ellie jumped the last set of tracks, confusion nearly making her stumble. "Dragged? By what?"

"A horse," Doctor Goodwin explained, having kept pace with them. Comprehension struck her then. Her stomach turned.

Broken bones, lacerations, puncture wounds, internal bleeding…her mind ticked off the possible injuries the man had sustained as they hurried west of the depot, along the tracks. She wasn't prepared, however, for what greeted her as they came down the embankment.

A man laid on his back in the snow-covered ballast. His clothes had been ripped to shreds, and what was left of them had been caked with mud and dirt and blood. Open lacerations scored his skin and oozed blood; one ear had been torn away completely; his lips were raw, showing broken teeth as he moaned; and his arm was visibly twisted and broken.

Ellie stared at the mess of the man's body and fought the urge to be sick.

"Holy hell," Doctor Goodwin murmured as he knelt beside the man.

"I found him like this," Rachel explained. Her voice trembled.

There was no time for emotion.

"There is nothing we can do here for him. He needs an infirmary," Ellie said. "Doctor Goodwin, where is the closest one?"

He nodded, taking in her question and breaking his horrified stare. "Doctor Jansen. It's on Fifth Street."

"Can you carry him there?" There was no way Ellie or Rachel would be able to. The man wasn't large, but he was bigger than either of them. Doctor Goodwin, on the other hand, was tall and muscular. To her relief, he was able to lift the man while Ellie braced his broken arm—the radius protruded through the skin at the elbow and appeared shattered.

"I'll run ahead," Rachel said, then darted away. Doctor Goodwin was slow moving, his burden awkward and moaning as he reached consciousness then fainted time and again.

As they came off the tracks and onto the first streets of Grantstown, a few women screamed, and some men stood back in alarm as Doctor Goodwin carried the bloodied man toward Fifth Street. Rachel had reached Doctor Jansen's offices quickly; as Ellie opened the door, the reporter was in the front hall and two attending nurses immediately indicated which room to enter. There was a sense of urgency in the small collection of rooms.

Doctor Goodwin had just laid him on a table when a portly, silver-haired man crashed through a swinging door.

"Hit by a train?" he asked.

"No, dragged by a horse, I think. Found by the tracks," Rachel corrected. She stood by a window, eyes darting out to the street. Ellie frowned, her worry rising. Did she think someone was watching?

Doctor Jansen circled the table, assessing the man through a pair of wire rimmed spectacles. "Who is he?"

Ellie bristled, her impatience mounting as the doctor kept his hands clasped behind his back and continued to inspect the man. If this were her infirmary, she would already be removing the man's clothes and setting to work on his injuries, starting with the arm.

"Not sure," Rachel said. She speared Ellie with a pleading stare. "I just stumbled across him down beyond the depot."

Was she lying to protect the man's identity? Ellie didn't care to argue.

"Very well. Out. All of you," the doctor barked.

Rachel fled the room, but Ellie stayed. "I'm happy to assist if you could use another hand."

The man was riddled with injuries; even with his two assistants, it would likely take the doctor hours to care for him on his own.

Doctor Jansen fumbled with the hem of his sleeve, popping the buttons to roll it up, and looked at Ellie out the top rim of his wire glasses. "Assist? Good god, woman, why on earth—"

His attention caught on her doctor's bag, and his scowl was so swift and fierce, Ellie nearly blanched.

"So. You're the child killer who's come west to hide, are you?"

The insult slapped her across the cheek. Ellie's throat closed off, stunned at the man's cruelty.

"That's uncalled for." Doctor Goodwin's deep voice startled Ellie almost as much as the affront had. He hadn't left the room as Rachel had.

"It's entirely appropriate, Henry, and well you know it. What are you doing associating with this woman?" Doctor Jansen sneered. He wouldn't even look at Ellie.

Mayor Carson had spread the word about the accident in Boston far and wide, it seemed. Even Doctor Goodwin had once told her that she should be wary of the mayor's influence. But even with that warning, she hadn't expected this level of derision.

"Doctor Jansen, while I understand your concern, I can assure you that I'm not trying to hide from my mistake back east."

"*Concern*? I don't concern myself with you at all, and I certainly won't have you in my operating room to assist. Out. Both of you."

He waved his arms as two of his nurses entered the room carrying linens and a tray of pristine steel instruments.

Doctor Goodwin took Ellie by the elbow and guided her toward the door. She could barely feel her own two feet as she walked in a haze. The brutal set-down had come so unexpectedly, so harshly, it left her breathless. She spilled out onto the sidewalk, where the wintery air snapped at her cheeks and stung her eyes. They teared, and Ellie swiftly blinked.

"I should have warned you about him." Doctor Goodwin stood next to her, his hand still on her arm. "He's a crotchety old goat, but his was the closest place."

She cleared her throat. "It doesn't matter, so long as he's able to help."

He turned and blocked the gusting wind some. "He was out of line."

"It's nothing I haven't dealt with a hundred times before," she said, unable to look at him. She didn't want him to see her wet eyes.

Rachel was already pacing a small swath of wooden board sidewalk, her hands on her hips. "I can't believe this happened," she said. "Hodge must have discovered Tom's plans to talk to Granger."

"Hodge?" Doctor Goodwin released Ellie's arm. For a

moment, she lamented the loss of it. But then shook off the ridiculous notion. "*Chet* Hodge?"

"One of his riders was willing to inform on him," Rachel confirmed.

Doctor Goodwin—or Henry, as Doctor Jansen had called him —cut off Rachel's next turn. "Do you have any idea how much danger you've put yourselves in? The man's a murderer."

Ellie's indignation toward Doctor Jansen vanished almost instantly. "Doctor Goodwin is right. And what if this Tom fellow had been in the middle of his meeting with Jack when Hodge found them?"

Ellie felt ill imagining what might have happened.

Rachel didn't stop pacing. She waved a hand, unconcerned. "Your sheriff knew what he was getting into. And there's no use carrying on about what *didn't* happen. We have a bigger problem now."

"You won't get your story," Ellie grumbled.

Rachel balked at her. "That's not fair! Everyone would have gotten something—Tom would get immunity, I'd get a story, and your sheriff would get his reputation restored."

Ellie stiffened. "He isn't *my* sheriff. He isn't sheriff at all."

She met Doctor Goodwin's gaze. He still looked disturbed and more than a little incensed. "I'm sorry. I didn't intend to involve you."

"That's who you were meeting at the Strike? An outlaw?"

Ellie started to explain that it was in fact Jack meeting with Tom but was cut off by the sound of her name being shouted down the street.

"Doc!"

She spun around, and relief made her weak-kneed as Jack reached her. He took her by her shoulders.

"Are you okay? You weren't at the Silver Strike and Billy said you left in a hurry."

He threw Doctor Goodwin a once-over before turning his anxious stare back to her.

"I'm fine," she said, warming at his concern.

"The same can't be said for my contact," Rachel added bitterly. She jerked her chin toward the infirmary door. "Hodge got to him."

Disappointment and fury darkened Jack's eyes. He swore under his breath and let Ellie go. "Dead?"

"Just about," Rachel replied.

"He might pull through," Ellie offered, though deep down she wasn't hopeful.

Jack grimaced, then faced Doctor Goodwin. "You're the pharmacist."

"Henry Goodwin," he introduced himself. He didn't extend a hand for a proper shake. Neither did Jack. In fact, Jack didn't say anything at all. He only continued to glower at him suspiciously.

"He helped us get Tom to Doctor Jansen," Ellie said, hoping the tone of her voice would hint at how misdirected Jack's anger was.

Resignation loosened Jack's shoulders and jaw. He turned to Ellie. "I'm going to stay in Grantstown for the night. If Tom pulls through, I'll want to talk to him."

"You can stay with me, Ellie, if you like," Rachel offered. But she shook her head.

"I shouldn't be away from the infirmary for too long." Not to mention that she was still upset with Rachel and her manipulation of Jack.

"You'll want to hurry for the next train then," Doctor Goodwin said.

Ellie half expected him to offer to walk her to the depot—he'd insisted on staying at the Silver Strike until her friends arrived, after all. But instead, he slipped back into his old broody and irascible character. He made a curt nod. "Doctor Lennox." And with that, he walked away.

Rachel whistled as he briskly departed. "Well, isn't he charming."

"Can you blame him?" Ellie rubbed her temple, an ache forming there. She hardly imagined that she'd encounter a situation like this when she left Sage Canyon that morning; Doctor Goodwin most certainly hadn't anticipated it.

Jack offered to take her to the depot, and though Ellie was more than capable of walking herself, she wouldn't turn down the opportunity to speak to him privately.

"If you speak to Tom and Hodge finds out, I'm worried what he might do," she said as soon as they'd left Rachel. She'd insisted on staying at the infirmary. Perhaps she'd sensed Ellie's irritation with her. "He's already killed two men, maybe three. And he knows how desperately you want to put him behind bars."

What didn't make sense was why Chet Hodge was regrouping now, after two years of being on the run.

"Don't worry about me," Jack said.

"I can't help it," she admitted. "I don't want anything to happen to you."

They reached the tracks and Jack took her hand, pulling her to a stop. He angled his head to look into her eyes. "I know how to handle myself with the likes of Hodge. Trust me." He brushed his thumb along the side of her chin, the leather of his glove cool. The familiar intimacy of the touch, however, flustered her.

"I wish I could ride back with you, doc. I don't like leaving you alone with Hodge so close by."

He'd said something like it before. But there was no reason for Hodge or his riders to consider Ellie at all, let alone target her. She wondered if Jack's worry wasn't just born from the senseless way in which he'd lost his wife. She'd been walking in town, minding her own business, when a bullet went astray and cut her down.

However, instead of feeling moved by Jack's worry, it troubled her. If she was correct, then it seemed Sarah was, once again, foremost on his mind.

Perhaps that was as it should be.

On the train ride back to Sage Canyon, she stared out the window, her eyes roaming over the trees lit by a fierce sunset. Jack confused her more than ever. Ellie touched her chin, where he'd run his thumb tenderly. He wouldn't have done that to Audrey or Myra, or any other woman…would he? And yet, he didn't want to move forward with a romance.

Her mind would have spun in circles if she let thoughts of Jack take over, so instead, she focused on her visit with Fiona. Ellie would at least be able to tell Audrey and Maggie that she was doing well.

As she at last climbed the front porch steps to McClure's, dusk settling over Sage Canyon in earnest, she thought of Doctor Goodwin too. It seemed each time they crossed paths, she learned something new and surprising about him. After today, however, she was positive he regretted running into her at the saloon.

What a mess it had all turned out to be.

CHAPTER 9

*S*leeping in was a luxury Ellie didn't often afford herself. Perhaps on her birthday or on Christmas morning she indulged, but most of the time, she was up with the sun. In Boston, that habit made her the odd duck out, with her mother and sister taking hours to rise, breakfast, dress, and get on with their day. That languid sort of pace had never appealed to Ellie.

However, the morning after her day in Grantstown, her eyes didn't crack open until the sun's rays had shifted far enough to shed over her pillow. It took a few moments to understand the position of the hands on the clock by her bed and then several more to comprehend that she'd slept through to the obscene hour of nine-thirty.

Pushing herself up onto her elbow, she rubbed the sleep out of her eyes and figured the extra hours of rest must have been needed. Her first thought was of Tom and if he'd made it through the night. Her second thought was of Jack. That thought was slightly more complicated, and Ellie didn't have the fortitude to give it the time it needed. She would require coffee and one of Audrey's hearty breakfasts first.

She'd just barely finished dressing when the swish of a skirt and quick feet sounded from the hallway, and then a rapid knock landed on her door.

"Doctor Ellie?" Maggie's panicked voice came through the wood.

Ellie whipped the door open. "What's wrong?"

"Come quickly. It's Myra, she's having trouble breathing." Maggie turned on her heel and rushed back down the hallway.

With practiced motions and speed, Ellie snatched her doctor's bag from where she always kept it, on the trunk at the base of her bed, and hurried to the kitchen.

When she'd been in medical college, one of her professors had stated that as physicians, they couldn't allow the human body's natural reaction of surprise, fear, or alarm to affect them. When they entered a troubling or unknown situation, the first and foremost requirement was calm and focus. Shaking hands and gasping breaths would only be a hindrance.

So, as Ellie entered the kitchen, she forced the sense of calm poise that she had been working to perfect ever since that professor's lesson. It wasn't always easy, but as she took in the scene— Myra, seated in a chair at the table with her head in her hands. Audrey at her side, rubbing circles on her back—Ellie took in the general atmosphere of the room. It was sadness, not danger.

"Myra?" Ellie set her doctor's bag on the table.

"She couldn't draw a full breath," Audrey supplied, just as Caleb entered the kitchen, carrying a quilt. Audrey thanked him and wrapped it around Myra's shoulders.

Ellie crouched in front of Myra, who lowered her hands. Her coloring was flushed, her eyes wet with tears. She sniffled.

"I'm sorry, Doctor Ellie, I think I just panicked."

A quick listen to her heart and lungs with her stethoscope and Ellie nodded to Audrey, silently assuring her that Myra was okay.

"Panicked, why?" Ellie asked. "Is it the baby?"

Myra shook her head. Her nostrils flared and her eyes filled again. "It's Nate," she said, her voice husky and strained.

"Nate?" Ellie looked to Audrey, whose downturned lips expressed dismay.

"He's gone," Myra hiccuped, and then started crying.

"Just for a little while," Audrey said. "He told Myra that it's safer for her and the baby to not be with him right now."

Ellie stood up and threw the stethoscope back into her bag. "Because of Chet Hodge?"

Myra sniffled and got to her feet too. "He's killing off old gang members and Nate thinks...he wonders...if my pa was shot by accident. Maybe whoever it was came for Nate?" She walked nervously toward the door, then stopped and turned back again. "I just don't understand! Why is he coming around here now? Why couldn't he and his lowlife friends just stay away?"

The reason why Hodge was re-forming his gang now eluded Ellie, but she suspected he was eliminating anyone who didn't care to join up again because they knew something they shouldn't. Tom had been planning to spill secrets to Jack and Rachel and look what had happened to him.

"Do you know where he's gone?" Ellie asked, thinking of the Silver Strike, where his father and Fiona were. But that would be too obvious, she supposed.

Myra shook her head, curling her hand into a fist and pressing it to her lips.

"He thought it would be safer if she didn't know," Audrey explained. "And I've insisted she stay here for the time being. There are plenty of rooms upstairs and that way, she's not alone...in case Hodge or his boys do come sniffing around again."

The thought of that slowed Ellie's pulse. No one spoke. Near the door to the hallway, Maggie and Caleb moved closer together.

"I'll make up a room for you," Maggie offered. Caleb, though he kept his eyes down, added, "I'll bring in wood for the stove."

"I don't know," Myra said. "I don't want to be a bother."

Audrey clasped her by the shoulders. "I would worry myself

sick if you didn't stay. Trust me, you're doing me a favor. And with the Christmas dance coming up, I could use some help in the kitchen. If you're up to it?"

Myra nodded, dabbing at her eyes again.

Ellie snapped her doctor's bag shut. "I think it's a good idea too."

Audrey turned to her on her way to the stove. "Did you get your telegram?"

Maggie made a gasping sound and reached into her skirt pocket. "Oh, I forgot to give it to you," she said, extending the small Western Union envelope.

Ellie snatched the telegram from her fingers, belatedly realizing how desperate she must have appeared. Slightly embarrassed, she opened it, and the tension in her shoulders and back instantly released.

"It's from Jack," she breathed, reading the abbreviated sentences. "He says Tom survived and that he's going to stay until he can speak to him." Ellie peered at Myra, who'd taken a seat again. "Did Nate ever speak about a man named Tom?"

She shook her head firmly. "Never. He didn't ever tell me anything about his time with the Hodge boys. He was too ashamed of it."

It had certainly seemed that way to Ellie too.

"What kind of trouble did the Hodge gang used to get up to before they disbanded?" Ellie asked next.

Myra rubbed her arms, as if chilled. She picked up the quilt she'd dropped and wrapped it around her shoulders again. "Robbery, mostly. They held up a few banks, raided cattle farms, waylaid supply trains. They mostly just took what they wanted and terrorized anyone who stood up to them."

If they were mostly robbers before, then that was likely what they would be getting up to again. But unless Jack managed to get anything out of Tom, there was no way of truly knowing.

"You missed breakfast, but I saved a little something for you,"

Audrey said, removing a pan of warmed eggs, bacon, and toast from the stove. The clench of Ellie's chest surprised her. Audrey's thoughtfulness was something she feared she'd never be able to repay.

"That's so kind of you," she said, the words feeling insufficient. Audrey really did take care of the people in her life.

After eating, and a cup of strong coffee, Ellie and Myra went back to the shop to collect some of her things for her stay.

It didn't take long to get her settled in, but she wasn't truly settled at all. Ellie found it hard to say anything helpful to calm Myra or assure her that her husband would be all right and home soon. He was surely doing what he thought best for his wife and unborn child, but at the same time, Myra was left with a whole load of uncertainty. At least she'd be at the boarding house where Ellie and Audrey could distract her.

It was past noon when Ellie finally walked to the post office, which was also the Western Union, and send a telegram to Jack's attention in the care of Doctor Jansen. If he was to be found anywhere in Grantstown, it would be at the infirmary. She informed him of Nate's leaving and requested an update on Tom's condition.

She was about to leave the Western Union when she a thought came to her, and she turned back to Mr. Yeaton. "I'd like to send a second wire."

She wrote out an abbreviated message to Doctor Goodwin—Henry—thanking him for his assistance and expressing an apology for such an unexpectedly hectic afternoon. The cost of the telegram was extravagant, and Ellie knew she really should be saving her pennies, especially since she didn't plan on asking her father for money to support her. However, Henry had been a real help, and his chivalrous gesture at the Silver Strike couldn't be shrugged off either.

The entire walk back to Green Street, she worried that perhaps sending a telegram had been too forward. There had been a few moments the day before when an awkwardness had started to build between them; a tension that Ellie hadn't really wanted to acknowledge then, though now that she'd sent that telegram, did.

She pushed the thought from her mind when she turned down Green Street and saw a bevy of people standing outside the infirmary door. A woman held the hand of a little boy, and a man and woman stood with a girl about the same age as the boy.

Guilt sluiced through her as she picked up her speed.

"I'm so sorry to have made you all wait," she said, climbing the porch steps and fishing through her pocket for her key. "I hope you haven't been here long?"

Of course, the one day she slept in would be the day her infirmary was overrun!

"Just five minutes or so," the mother of the little boy answered. "Charlie's had a cough and a fever since yesterday morning."

"Violet, too," the man said, whipping off his hat as the group of them entered the infirmary at the same time. "And she's got a rash."

"Charlie too!" the mother exclaimed.

Ellie peeled off her coat and rushed to put on a pinafore. "A rash?" Her pulse slowed, then sped again. "I'll take a look at Violet first. On the table if you will."

Her father lifted her onto the table and after feeling her lymph nodes, which were badly swollen, Ellie took a peek down the collar of her dress. Red blotches speckled her chest and back.

Sweat built up on Ellie's neck as she asked Violet to open her mouth and say, "Ahh." Worry spiked low into her stomach at the sight of her strawberry tongue, patched with white.

Violet's parents and then Charlie's mother watched with trepidation as Ellie quickly checked the little boy too. His tongue didn't have quite the same level of red-and-white splotch that Violet did, but it still looked like a ripe strawberry plucked from a field. His rash covered his back more than his front.

She took their temperatures though she knew before the mercury rose that they would ring in at no less than 103 degrees. She gave each child a peppermint candy and then took their parents aside.

"Is it diphtheria?" Violet's mother asked, her hands clasped tightly, her knuckles white. It made Ellie think of Dottie Winthrop and her little girl Lulu, who'd she'd seen in here just the other day.

"No, I don't believe so," Ellie answered. "All their symptoms point to scarlet fever."

Charlie's mother nodded. "I wondered if that was it. My sister and I caught it when we were young. I remember the rashes."

Ellie's mind spun forward. She forced herself to breathe evenly as she planned her next steps. "Do they go to school?"

The parents nodded.

"I'll need to see all their classmates, and we'll have to establish a quarantine immediately for all the children who've contracted it."

"You mean we can't take Violet home?" her mother asked, eyes wide and shining now.

"I wouldn't recommend it. Scarlet fever is highly contagious, and to stop the spread of the bacteria, it's best to contain it to one space."

Though, where to set up the quarantine? She looked around her small infirmary. It was enough space for Charlie and Violet, but if there were more sick children, it wouldn't do.

"Mister…?" Ellie said, turning to Violet's father. She realized, belatedly, that she hadn't been introduced.

"Thackery," he said. "Dan Thackery. This is my wife, Julia."

"I wondered if you might come with me to the children's school. I haven't properly met their schoolteacher, Mrs. Newsom yet. I'd like to see if any other children were kept home today."

It was decided that Violet and Charlie would stay at the infirmary with their mothers while Ellie and Mr. Thackery walked across town to the schoolhouse, which operated out of a barn next to the livery. As they approached, Ellie could hear a woman's voice coming from inside. There were a few windows, through which children could be seen at desks, and an older woman wrote on a freestanding blackboard.

Ellie buried her dislike of Mrs. Newsom as Mr. Thackery rolled open the barn door. The older woman's lesson cut off mid-sentence. She slapped a pointer she was holding into her opposite palm, causing Ellie and the students to jump.

"May I help you?" the teacher bit out sharply.

Ellie cleared her throat. "Mrs. Newsom, I'm Doctor Ellie Lennox—"

"I know who you are."

The class had all turned in their seats to look at their unexpected visitors. Ellie bore the woman's instant hostility with a forced grin.

"I was hoping to speak to you," she went on. Then, after Mrs. Newsom stared blankly at her, added, "In private."

One of the teacher's dark silver brows arched. "I am in the middle of a lesson, Miss Lennox."

"This is urgent." Ellie wouldn't say anything in front of the children, as they would likely panic and be afraid. She only hoped their teacher would tread carefully too.

With flared nostrils, Mrs. Newsom stared Ellie down a moment before addressing the class. "Continue working on your arithmetic problems while I see to this."

She bustled toward Ellie with dragon-like irritation. Mr. Thackery cowed visibly under her stare as she reached them.

"What is the meaning of this interruption?" she said, though not in a tone that would escape the ears of her listening pupils.

Ellie motioned for them to move closer to the barn door, which Mr. Thackery had rolled shut to keep out the cold air.

When the teacher stood firm, Ellie sighed and lowered her voice. "Mrs. Newsom, two of your students are in my infirmary right now, including Violet Thackery and another little boy, Charlie."

The woman's lips thinned. "There is a cold making its way through the town, Miss Lennox. Hardly an emergency."

Ellie kept her voice lowered. "I'm afraid these two children have scarlet fever."

A flicker of concern wrinkled her brow. Otherwise, her grim expression didn't change. "Are you certain it's scarlatina?"

The question was one of doubt, not concern.

"Yes, quite certain. It's highly contagious. Are there any other children in your class who appear ill today?"

"If they were ill, they would not be here."

That wasn't necessarily true. Ellie could tell Mrs. Newsom was simply trying to be argumentative. As one of Muriel Carson's friends, it was clear why.

"I ask that you send any child who appears feverish or has a sore throat, or begins to develop a rash, to my infirmary—"

"I certainly will not," she bit out. Ellie jerked back, stunned at her vehemence. "Most parents in this town do not wish for you to treat their children, and for very good reason."

She'd known the sentiment was out there but hearing it direct from the schoolteacher's lips cut into her like a sharp knife. Ellie braced herself, clenching her teeth against a response that would only fan the flames higher.

Calm, Ellie. Calm.

"Be that as it may, scarlet fever is not to be trifled with. I'm establishing a quarantine for those children who show symptoms. It is paramount that they be separated from other children, to try and reduce the spread of infection."

Mrs. Newsom's severe stare snapped to Mr. Thackery and asked, incredulously, "Mrs. Thackery has agreed to let her treat dear Violet?"

Mr. Thackery, though intimidated, replied, "Can't take a chance, not after what happened last winter."

Mrs. Newsom held her tongue and jutted her doughy chin. The mention of the diphtheria outbreak must have shaken a bone of sympathy loose within the older woman, for she finally blew out a frustrated huff of air and said, "I will inform the parents of your quarantine, but I cannot make them come to you, Miss Lennox. Now, I need to return to my lesson."

It was all Ellie was going to get, that much was clear. As she and Mr. Thackery left the schoolhouse, her muscles quivered uncontrollably from the tense confrontation.

"Gracious," she breathed out. "That woman really is a dragon."

He laughed but didn't argue. "I can go 'round to a few homes and let some mothers know about the fever."

Ellie brightened. "Would you? That would be wonderful, Mr. Thackery. I know Mrs. Newsom wasn't exaggerating when she said there were many parents who don't wish for me to treat their children, but—"

"Oh, well, now, she might have been exaggerating just a little," he cut in with another light laugh. "Audrey McClure's got a whole lotta sway with the townsfolk, you know, and she sets store by you. Cameron family, too, after what you did for them. I reckon any child who shows symptoms will turn up at your door."

With a tip of his hat, Mr. Thackery walked off in the opposite direction, on his mission. Ellie stared after him with astonishment. A bubbling of warm joy—despite the circumstances—buoyed her. If what he said was true, perhaps with time, more townspeople would feel comfortable coming to her infirmary.

As she made her way back to Green Street, she just hoped that for now those parents with sick children chose to come to her sooner rather than later.

CHAPTER 10

*B*y early that evening, two more children had turned up on the front porch of the infirmary. A brother and sister had gone home from Mrs. Newsom's schoolhouse with fevers and sore throats. As Mr. Thackery had already made a round of calls on some homes, the children's father, a widower named Mr. Burnham, knew about Violet and Charlie and the importance of going straight to Doc Ellie.

However, it quickly become apparent that the infirmary was no place for a proper quarantine. Violet and Charlie had been settled onto the two beds Ellie had outfitted the infirmary with, however the additional two children had nothing but their father's lap and a makeshift pallet on the infirmary's rug, next to the potbelly stove. Not to mention the noise coming through the adjoining wall. The Canary was growing louder by the hour. Dade rolled his eyes when she asked if it could be possible to keep the noise down just for tonight.

"Trust me, doc, it'll get a helluva lot louder if I dare ask my patrons to shut their yappers."

Dade had stood far back from the adjoining door, having

heard about the scarlet fever patients inside. He was right, of course. The only option would be to find a new location for the quarantine.

"I could put them in a few rooms at the hotel," Audrey offered when she stopped by with a pot of still-steaming chicken stew. How she managed to whip up the most perfect food for the moment continued to astonish Ellie, as did her generosity. But she couldn't take Audrey up on the offer.

"It needs to be a space totally closed off from the public. I also don't want Maggie or Caleb anywhere near the children. Or Myra," Ellie added as the two of them stood on the infirmary's front porch.

She hadn't allowed Audrey inside, either. Though the fever mostly affected children, adults weren't immune. Ellie didn't want to take any chances.

After a moment of thought, Audrey had brightened. "What about Frank's store? It isn't being used, what with Myra staying at the boarding house for the moment."

It was a good idea, and Myra approved it immediately when Audrey hastened back to McClure's to ask her. So, with help from Caleb, Mr. Thackery, and even a bothered Dade, Audrey organized the quarantine inside Eberly's store. They set up a few cots and mattresses, started the woodstove, pumped well water into buckets, and Audrey and Maggie and Katherine Toft brought over enough food and blankets to provide for the children. Only when everyone cleared out of the prepared shop did Ellie and the parents transfer the children to their new quarters. Using a nub of charcoal, Ellie wrote "Quarantine" upon a white linen towel from the infirmary and hung it in the window. She also left a note in the door at the infirmary, directing parents to the new dedicated space.

It took a while for the stove to warm the shop, but the children were much more comfortable there in the quiet space with their beds surrounding the potbelly stove. It was nearly seven in the evening when Ellie thought to telegram Doctor Goodwin yet again and request a shipment of antipyretics. As there was no medicinal cure for scarlet fever, there wouldn't be much she could do other than administer small doses of phenacetin to reduce their fevers and make them more comfortable.

When Ellie returned to the shop from the telegraph office, she came to a halt in the open doorway. Tamora was seated next to Violet on a stool. On the other side of Violet's bed, Mr. Thackery was laying out a makeshift pallet on the floor. Charlie's mother sat next to her little boy, darning some clothes while he slept. Sam, an eleven-year-old boy, and Lucy, his six-year-old sister, lay on cots right next to one another. Their father, Mr. Burnham was the local ferrier, and was raising them alone after their mother died giving birth to Lucy.

"Might want to shut that door," Tamora said, her palm pressed against the little girl's forehead.

Ellie snapped out the cold, hearing the glass rattle in the pane.

"Parents have to stay," Tamora said. "And you should too, doc. No more running out of here."

Ellie gritted her teeth against the admonishment. "I know how to organize a quarantine." Looking at Violet and Mr. Thackery again, she wondered where Mrs. Thackery was. Her husband must have read Ellie's mind.

"My wife had to go home. We've got three other little ones, youngest is an infant."

Ellie nodded, praying the other Thackery children wouldn't come down with symptoms of the fever.

"I told Mrs. Thackery she should keep to the house for now," Tamora said as Ellie unwrapped herself from her heavy wool coat and peeled off her mittens. The shop was still chilled, so she moved closer to the stove. Violet's prickly red rash had spread up the sides of her throat, toward her ears.

"How did you hear about the outbreak?" Ellie asked the midwife.

"I was at Toft's for my newspapers," she answered.

Tamora often fed her stove with the old newspapers Katherine didn't sell at the mercantile. Last fall, when she'd found Boston broadsides in Tamora's kindling wood box, Ellie had suspected the midwife had been the one who'd slipped a cryptic note under the infirmary door, telling Ellie that she knew the truth about Todd Andrews. However, it had been Katherine who'd written the note in an attempt to warn Ellie that her father was about to let loose with what he'd discovered.

"I've administered phenacetin to help bring down their fevers, but I was hoping you might have some experience with scarlet fever?" Ellie asked while checking on Charlie and then Sam and Lucy.

"I've brought meadowsweet and willow bark tea," Tamora answered as she dipped a cloth into a bowl of cool water and wrung it out before placing it back on Violet's head. "The willow bark will keep them sleepy, so they'll rest, on top of clearing out their lungs and fighting infection."

"That's good, thank you. But do you?" Ellie pressed. "Have experience with scarlet fever?"

Tamora lifted her dark brown eyes and met Ellie's hopeful stare. She sighed heavily. Then stood up and jerked her chin away from Violet and her father. Ellie's stomach dipped. If Tamora wanted to talk to her away from the others, it couldn't be good news.

Once they were closer to Frank Eberly's old, scarred counter-top, Tamora whispered in her raspy voice, "The quarantine is wise. I've seen this illness rage out of control, and it's usually because parents don't understand how contagious the disease is."

Ellie hitched her breath, surprised. Tamora's support of a quarantine was most unexpected. She usually fought against Ellie's ideas.

"Oh. Well, thank you," Ellie stammered. "In Boston, when there was an outbreak, we'd set the children in a separate ward."

Tamora's lined brow puckered, as if she'd had a troubling thought.

"What is it?" Ellie asked.

She peered over her shoulder, at the resting children. "Too many succumbed to the diphtheria last winter. I worry."

It was understandable. Ellie touched Tamora's arm. "I'm worried too. But I'm glad you're here to help."

Now, it was Tamora's turn to look flabbergasted. She turned away before Ellie could fully see the answering grin that stretched her lips.

The two of them worked in tandem for the next few hours, preparing willow bark and meadowsweet tea, and cooling feverish foreheads with linens soaked in chilled water. Ellie had chiseled off a hunk of ice from inside Myra's icebox in the small kitchen, located at the back of the shop. As she went from cot to cot, she felt the tug of impatience. How she wished there was medicine to cure diseases like this. Advancements were being made, but not fast enough.

At midnight, after the children and their parents had fallen into an uneasy asleep, a knock sounded on the shop's front door. Ellie's heart crashed inside her chest.

She opened the door a slim crack to find Mr. and Mrs. Booker, each of them holding a sleepy child.

"Bobby's got a fever," Mrs. Booker said breathlessly.

"Graham is just tired," Mr. Booker added, indicating the little boy he carried. The child's eyes were closed as he rested his head on his father's shoulder.

"Mr. Booker, if you enter the quarantine, you'll have to stay. Will the mine allow you time off?" Ellie asked, wishing she could have said something less rigid.

He looked at his wife and gave a solemn shake of his head. "Can't give the foreman any reason to cut me loose."

Ellie had met the foreman before and had disliked him immensely. Mr. Booker's regret and frustration was nearly palpable as he transferred the sleeping Graham to Ellie's arms, gave his wife a peck on the cheek, and then rubbed Bobby's back tenderly.

The Bookers exchanged a worried look. Ellie tried not to read too much into the shared glance. Were they upset to be here, resorting to asking Ellie for her help? Mrs. Booker's rejection last fall had bothered her most out of everyone else in Sage Canyon. She supposed it didn't matter now though. A sick child was a sick child, and Ellie would do whatever she could to see him through.

"We'll be okay," Mrs. Booker assured him, and with a clench of her stomach, Ellie hoped she was right.

"Over here," Ellie said, pointing to an empty cot, one of a few she'd set up in case more patients arrived overnight. "Does he have a sore throat?"

Mrs. Booker nodded as she settled Bobby onto the cot. She then reached for Graham as Tamora appeared with a quilt and draped it over Bobby. Ellie's palm burned when she felt his forehead. His glands were swollen and hard, too.

"There doesn't seem to be a rash yet, but he is certainly ill," Ellie said, removing the stethoscope from his chest. His heart rate was slightly increased, normal for a body fighting an infection. She peered up at Bobby's younger brother Graham, still sleep on his mother's shoulder.

"You can settle him on another cot for the night. I hope I'm wrong, but it's possible he will develop a fever too. I'll check on him in the morning."

For now, she would let him have his rest.

The long night dragged on, Ellie and Tamora taking turns resting on one of the cots while the other kept watch over the children. As dawn's light slowly brightened the shop, Ellie decided it was high time someone made a pot of coffee. Seeing how Audrey was back at McClure's, she figured it was up to her. She did her best, but the finished product smelled burnt and tasted burnt too.

Tamora wrinkled her nose. "I'll make tea."

Ellie nodded. "Good idea."

They didn't have to wait very long after the sun rose for Audrey to show up at their door. Ellie, wrapping her shawl around her shoulders, slipped outside and smelled a decadent breakfast—including the aroma of well brewed coffee. Audrey held a large, covered basket.

"You're an angel," Ellie sighed.

Audrey laughed. "I'm well rested, which you are not." She peered into Ellie's eyes. "Did you sleep at all?"

She shook her head. "Mr. and Mrs. Booker arrived last night. Bobby is ill."

Audrey handed her the basket. "I'll bring lunch later. Maggie is already working on cornbread biscuits."

"I don't know what I'd do without you," Ellie said.

Her friend's eyes glinted with humor, something Ellie was grateful to see after such a long, tense night. "You'd do exactly what you're doing—healing people, the way you're meant to," she replied, and with a squeeze of Ellie's shoulder, she turned and started back for McClure's.

As she watched her go, she hoped Audrey was right. Scarlet fever patients did not always heal, and Tamora's hushed worry the night before had stayed with Ellie like a low fog in her mind that refused to clear out. What if one of the parents took ill? Or, throughout the day, the quarantine become flooded with more sick patients? Ellie closed her eyes. Worrying ahead of time would not fix anything. She had to keep her mind clear and calm.

Inside, the children were slowly waking. Coughs and complaints started up, and Audrey's delicious breakfast of scrambled eggs and buttered toast only distracted them for a short while. Katherine, having acute foresight, had brought a few books from the mercantile for the children the day before, and it turned out that Mrs. Booker was rather good at reading to a crowd, her voice lilting and animated in all the right places. So, while she sat with Bobby and entertained the children who could keep their eyes open, Ellie poured herself a second tin mug of Audrey's coffee. She let it warm her palms as she leaned against the countertop and took a moment to breathe. At least little Graham had not yet developed a fever or sore throat. He sat on the cot next to his brother's, stretching his neck to try to look at the book's illustrations.

Motion at the shop's front door brought a hitch of dread into the base of Ellie's throat. Another patient? The linen towel bearing the charcoaled quarantine sign hung in the glass, obscuring everything but the man's broad shoulders. As Ellie approached the door, familiarity rushed over her. Her heart stuttered with astonishment as she swung open the door and looked up into Henry Goodwin's face.

"Doctor Goodwin?" Her voice pitched higher with surprise. "I didn't expect to see you here."

He wore a thick, gray wool coat and gray bowler, and in one hand, he held a large leather case. Two lines creased the space between his dark brows as he lifted his attention to the inside of the shop.

"I took the nine o'clock," he said succinctly. His deep voice was even lower and rougher to her ears this morning.

She'd telegrammed last evening requesting medicines, not the pharmacist himself.

"I...I see that, but, well, it wasn't necessary to deliver them personally," she said, then realizing it sounded a bit rude, added, "Though I do appreciate the effort—"

"I have the serum."

Ellie blinked up at him. "Serum?"

"The diphtheria antitoxin."

Excitement shot through her. She quickly stepped aside, but Henry only had one foot through the door when she remembered something.

"Oh!" She jammed her hand against his chest and gave him a shove. He stumbled back and peered down at her, bewildered. Ellie quickly explained, "But this is a scarlet fever quarantine, not diphtheria."

"Yes, but it's been observed that diphtheria is a complication of scarlet fever. The two are related. Perhaps the treatment could be effective."

Ellie's excitement crested again, but then held. "But the quarantine...if you enter—"

"I'll have to stay. Yes, I know," he said impatiently. He looked over her shoulder again. "May I?"

The vibrations of his voice reached through her palm, straight up into the bones of her fingers. With a gasp, she realized she still held her hand flat against his chest and pulled it away.

He cocked a brow. "I intend to stay, Doctor Lennox. I pulled all the strings I could to get my hands on a few bottles of the antitoxin. Do you know how to dispense it?"

Ellie shook her head. She'd never even seen a bottle of the newly developed antitoxin. "You could contract the fever."

"Highly unlikely. I had it as a boy, so I stand a good chance at being immune." He winced as a gust of cold wind barreled down the street and whipped at his back.

She bit the inside of her lip, apprehensive still. His immunity was likely, yes, but the quarantine could be in place for a week or more. "Surely you can't stay away from your shop for days and days?"

"There are two other pharmacists in Grantstown," he said, then narrowing his eyes on her, "Doctor Lennox, I'm getting the impression you don't want me here."

She straightened and flushed. "No, of course not!" But she stumbled over what to say next. It wasn't that she didn't want him here; it was the odd fact that seeing him at the door and hearing that he'd be staying had given her a slightly jittery sensation. One that baffled her.

Before she could say anything further to embarrass herself or insult him, she sealed her lips and stood aside, swinging out an arm to usher him inside. He entered the shop, and immediately, his spectacles fogged up. Ellie tried to stifle a laugh as he whipped them off.

Her amused half-grin froze in place. Without his glasses, Henry appeared…well…*different*. She didn't know how to explain it, really. His face looked unfamiliar all the sudden, and yet also striking. When he put his de-fogged spectacles on again, she shook away the unsettling thoughts.

"Would you like coffee?" she asked.

He brought his leather case to the long countertop, placing it on its side next to Frank's empty and abandoned cash till. "Thank you, yes."

She poured him the last of Audrey's coffee as he opened the case, revealing what looked like a miniature apothecary. Three brown glass bottles were secured into place with wire clasps. Several clear glass bottles filled with various powders, each labeled in neat writing, were also secured. A mortar and pestle, measuring spoons, glass vials, and an assortment of other tools were secured into molded spaces too.

He pulled a brown bottle from a wire clasp. "It's a limited supply, but we're lucky to have even one bottle," he said, holding it up for her to see.

Tamora had exited the kitchen with another pot of willow bark tea and now came toward the open leather apothecary case.

"Doctor Goodwin has a new antitoxin," Ellie explained before Tamora could ask.

Her expression remained staid. "New? You plan to experiment on the children?"

Henry's expression remained steady and confident. "If we'd had this serum last winter, it would have saved lives."

Tamora brightened. "It's for diphtheria?"

"Officially, yes," he said, as if bracing for an argument like the one Ellie had given him. But Tamora only nodded succinctly.

"If it helps reduce the swelling of the throat, it will be useful."

She then left to dole out the tea.

"My thoughts, exactly," Henry said, sounding surprised that he hadn't needed to launch into an explanation.

Ellie eyed the small bottle in his hand. It had to be less than three ounces. "How many doses will these bottles provide?"

He took a deep breath. "A dozen at the most."

In a town the size of Sage Canyon, that may be enough. But then, what happened if they needed more? Or if a diphtheria outbreak occurred?

Ellie had a thought. "Are there any cases in Grantstown?"

He shook his head. "Not one."

"And there could be no adverse side effects? Using an anti-toxin designed for another illness?"

He hesitated, his fingers closing around the bottle. His hands looked strong, as if he could have been a wood carver or carpenter, rather than a druggist. Goodness, why was she ogling his hands? Ellie looked up and met his steady gaze.

"None that I can foresee. But you're the physician here," he said. "It's up to you if we use the antitoxin."

Taking a look around at the resting children, at their glazed eyes and sweaty skin, peppered with coarse red rashes, she nodded. "I want to. I just don't want to give the parents false hope."

Henry cupped her elbow with the hand not holding the serum bottle. His fingers felt as strong as they'd appeared. "I don't believe you ever would."

His gray green eyes held hers. She remembered the first time she'd met him, and how arrogant and prickly he'd been toward her. Shamelessly rude. Ellie had experienced everything from passive sarcasm to open hostility as she'd gone through medical school, then her initial years practicing, and ultimately, during the scandal that erupted in Boston. However, the Grantstown druggist had riled her like no other ever had. The reason why had eluded her then, and now, so did the reason this earnest remark filled her with an unexpected warmth.

He dropped his gaze to the cup of coffee she still held. "That for me?"

She'd forgotten all about the coffee. Belatedly, she thrust it toward him, splashing a little over the rim. She cringed inside. What was the matter with her?

Henry accepted the tin mug with a twitch of his lips, as though he could see just how flustered she was, and it amused him.

Ellie stepped back. "When do we begin?"

She was ready, even if the experimentation worried her. But if Henry believed the antitoxin could help, she was willing to try it. When they approached Mr. Thackery, Mrs. Booker, and the other parents, they all nodded. Scarlet fever was nearly as deadly as diphtheria, and though he was from Grantstown, they knew Henry and trusted him.

Ellie watched him prepare the syringe soon after receiving the parents' permission. He'd shed his overcoat and hat and rolled the cuffs on his shirt to the middle of his forearms. Her eyes drifted to the muscles on display as he inserted the needle into the vial and drew on the plunger. He commentated all the while, rattling off dosage numbers and reciting research he'd studied on the preparation of the antitoxin. Ellie wondered if he wasn't a bit anxious about the possible results; she knew she was. She also didn't like how the sight of his powerfully built forearms unnerved her. His presence shouldn't be affecting her in this manner. Especially not inside a scarlet fever quarantine.

Setting her head straight, Ellie suggested they begin with the oldest patient, eleven-year-old Sam. Henry handed her the needle and syringe, and Ellie sat on the edge of the boy's cot. She lowered the needle when the boy's eyes widened in fear. She suspected he had never seen a needle in his life.

"It'll be a small pinch of pain, Sam. And then, it will be over." Ellie leaned a little closer to whisper, "You're the eldest here, and the other children will look to you for guidance. Can you show them to be brave?"

Sam glanced at his little sister, whose rash had climbed up her neck and cheeks. Her lips appeared more swollen than they had been that morning at breakfast. He took a deep breath and nodded.

Ellie moved quickly, piercing the boy's skin on his shoulder, emptying the syringe, and withdrawing all within a single breath. Sam winced and his eyes watered, but he crinkled his nose and shrugged as Henry stealthily took the used needle from her hand.

"That wasn't so bad," Sam said. Ellie smiled widely, admiring the boy's spirit as she pressed a square of cotton to a bead of blood.

She returned to Henry at the countertop, which he'd transformed into a work counter. "What now?"

"I think we wait to see if there are any immediate adverse effects." He said this softly, so there could be no chance of anyone overhearing.

She prayed the next half hour or so would be uneventful. To her relief, it was, and she and Henry continued injecting the serum into the children at a slow rate, watching for any complications as they progressed. Audrey and Maggie knocked on the window just after noon, indicating that they were leaving the promised lunch baskets on the ground outside. The whole shop buzzed with activity, and though the serum had been administered, Ellie and Tamora continued with teas and poultices and cool cloths for feverish foreheads.

Two more children arrived, both from Mrs. Newsom's classroom, and once they were settled in, their parents approved the antitoxin injection.

Late afternoon sunlight was slipping behind the mountains when Ellie finally took a seat on a chair behind the counter. Her legs throbbed, her back ached, and her stomach rumbled. She hadn't stopped to eat any of the food delivered hours ago. All she wanted to do right then, however, was close her eyes. Just for a moment.

A throat cleared, and Ellie sat forward, opening her eyes again. Mrs. Booker stood before her, a small white enamel plate in her hand.

"I noticed you didn't eat," she said softly, extending the plate toward Ellie. A thick, flaky biscuit had been slathered with butter and blackberry preserves.

Ellie started to stand.

"No, sit," Mrs. Booker said quickly. "You need the rest. I just wanted to let you know that Bobby's feeling much better. Tamora says his glands feel smaller."

Relief coursed through her as she settled the plate on her lap. It had been warmed on the stovetop, she noticed. "I'm so happy to hear that. Have you told Doctor Goodwin?"

Picturing his thrilled reaction made Ellie grin. He'd been circling the shop methodically, feeling foreheads and glands, watching for responses to the serum.

"Yes." She hesitated, as if she wanted to say more.

"And Graham, is he still feeling well?"

"Oh yes, right as rain. Doctor Goodwin says he would have shown symptoms by now if he'd caught the bacteria," she said.

Unable to restrain herself another second, Ellie bit into the warm biscuit. Heaven seemed to explode over her tongue, and with a bit of horror, she realized she'd moaned in delight. Mrs. Booker only laughed.

"Audrey has some kind of magic in the kitchen," she said.

Then, Mrs. Booker clasped her hands before her. "Doctor Ellie, I owe you an apology."

Ellie choked down the biscuit and sat forward again. "No, please don't."

Mrs. Booker held up her hand. "Let me say my piece."

Ellie hinged her jaw and nodded.

After a long, weary sigh, Mrs. Booker began. "When we were younger, my parents brought my brother to a doctor. A white doctor in Richmond, Virginia. He grumbled about treating a black boy but my daddy, he was a driver for Mr. Lavoy, and Mr. Lavoy was a rich man. One of the wealthiest, in fact. Well, David had stomach pain and he was feverish, but the doctor, though he agreed to see David, said it was just indigestion. Sent him home."

Ellie furrowed her brow, suspecting what had happened. Mrs. Booker continued, confirming her guess.

"His appendix burst that night. Sepsis set in and he...he died."

Ellie closed her eyes, imagining the anguish Mrs. Booker and her family had endured. "I'm so sorry."

The doctor had dismissed David and his medical emergency out of irritation, and most certainly prejudice.

"I knew you were a good doctor before I learned about that boy you treated, but I let something that happened in my past, something that didn't have anything to do with you, stop me from trusting you."

Ellie set the plate on the counter and stood so she could be face to face with Mrs. Booker. "I don't hold that against you. In fact, I am the one who needs to apologize. If I could start over in Sage Canyon, I'd be forthright about what happened in Boston. I thought I could put it all behind me, as obtuse as that now seems."

Mrs. Booker chuckled. "We're all a little obtuse at times." She straightened her shoulders and let out a breath. "We all deserve a second chance too."

A weight lifted from her chest as Mrs. Booker gave one more

smile and nod, and then left to return to Bobby's cot. A second chance was exactly what Ellie had been given. A knot of worry looped low in her stomach. If the antitoxin didn't work, she didn't know if she'd be given a third chance. Yes, as a doctor, she only wielded so much power against something as brutal as scarlet fever, but she couldn't help but think the townsfolk would search for something—or someone—to blame.

CHAPTER 11

$\mathcal{B}$y nightfall, Bobby, Sam, his younger sister Lucy, Charlie, and the two newest patients, Timothy and Isaac, age eight and ten respectively, had started to visibly improve. Throats less painful, fevers reduced, they still scratched at the red, scaly rash along their necks, chests, faces, and shoulders, but their glands were no longer hard and swollen like before. The antitoxin had seemed to take effect in the way Henry had hoped, and cautious smiles were inching across most of the parents' faces.

All except Mr. Thackery's. Little Violet remained feverish, her glands swollen, her face puffy and red. Ellie took her temperature every quarter hour and it remained just over 103 degrees. No amounts of ice-cold cloths or willow bark tea seemed to be helping either. Fear had replaced the worry on Mr. Thackery's face, and Ellie felt it too, deep in the center of her chest.

"She isn't responding to the serum." Henry had joined Ellie at the long counter where she was dipping the much-used glass thermometer into a jar of carbolic acid to sterilize it. He had lowered his voice to a murmur so not to let Violet's father overhear.

"With a fever that high, lasting for so long a period, I worry she'll develop acute rheumatic fever," Ellie replied, also in a near whisper. The secondary infection would cause damage to her heart. If she survived, her health would never be the same.

Henry didn't say anything right away, and she peered up at him. He stared hard at the jar of carbolic acid, though his eyes were distant. "What is it?" she asked.

He blinked and hitched his chin. In that moment, Ellie witnessed an expression he had not yet worn, at least not in her presence: open vulnerability. He shuttered it quickly with his usual solemnity.

"Nothing. It's just…it's a devastating infection," he said, his voice raspy. He cleared his throat and quickly met her eyes before looking away again. There was something else. Something more.

"I had a patient in Boston who developed it," she said, hoping it would encourage Henry to say what he was thinking about. His interest was immediate.

"What was the outcome?"

"The child survived but…only for a short while. The damage to his heart was too severe."

It had not been the first child to die in the hospital ward in which she worked, but it had still stolen the breath from her lungs for what felt like days.

Henry crossed his arms. The black sleeve garters he wore cut into the brawny muscles of his upper arms.

"It doesn't only damage the heart, but the brain as well," he said.

Ellie perked. "You sound like a physician."

He grimaced and shook his head. "I prefer to work with medicines, not people."

"I don't know about that. You were very good with the parents and children today."

He gave her a sidelong glance that hinted that he didn't

believe her. But Ellie *had* thought he'd done well. Not one irritated or arrogant comment had tumbled from his mouth while the parents had asked questions and the children had sniffled and whimpered.

"How do you know about acute rheumatic fever?" she asked, unwilling to let it go just yet.

He leaned forward, bracing his forearms and elbows against the counter. "My sister, Margaret." He turned his head toward Ellie. "We both contracted scarlet fever when we were children."

He'd mentioned his probable immunity first thing that morning, but Ellie hadn't thought of it for the rest of the day. It had been far too hectic around the quarantine.

"She developed the secondary infection?" she presumed. Henry nodded, and Ellie's heart sank. She was almost afraid to ask her next question. "How did she fare?"

"She survived," he said, exhaling a breath. "But there were complications. Margaret wasn't the same after. Her brain and her heart have been impaired ever since. She never grew up, really. Still lives with my parents in Lancaster."

It was both a blessing and a curse. To survive only to emerge altered, incapable of leading an independent life... Before she knew what she was doing, Ellie had set her hand on his forearm. He eyed the touch with the same surprise Ellie herself felt, and she quickly retracted her hand.

"I'm sorry. About your sister," she added, any hope of covering the awkward gaffe now flying out the door. But Henry didn't appear to notice.

He straightened up, impressing his height upon Ellie once again. "We could try another dose of the serum, increasing it slightly," he began to say, but at that moment, a muffled cry came from the collection of cots in the center of the shop floor.

Awareness scattered over Ellie's shoulders and down her back, raking along her scalp as she looked toward Violet's cot.

Tamora hovered over her, one hand trying to hold Mr. Thackery back a step.

"Doc." Tamora's strong voice cut through the room. Ellie flew around the corner of the counter, toward the cot.

"Her breathing is shallow," Tamora said as Ellie reached her. She placed the stethoscope drum to the little girl's chest and listened. Her heartbeat was slow, and the strident rattle of each inhalation alarming.

"She isn't getting enough air," Ellie announced. She searched her mind for a solution as the world closed in around her; there was nothing that mattered more than getting air into Violet's lungs.

Henry crouched next to the cot. "Another dose of the serum could help."

Ellie shook her head. It had taken an hour or more for the other children to respond. Violet didn't have that long. She needed oxygen, *now*.

"It's too late for that," she said, "and she might not even respond to a second dose. No, there has to be another method."

Ellie felt the child's enflamed glands, her burning hot skin. With a tongue depressor, she then inspected the inside of her mouth. Violet's throat was nearly swollen shut.

"A procedure for diphtheria patients is a scraping of the suffo-cating membrane that develops over the airway," Ellie said, her mind racing. "It's messy and painful, and one of two last resorts to open a passageway to the lungs. Since there is no membrane here to scrape, I wonder…"

Ellie went still. Her mind knew, even if she didn't want to face it just yet.

"Doc?" Mr. Thackery prodded. Mrs. Booker had come to hold him by the shoulders, as if her strength alone could keep him in a standing position.

Ellie met his fearful eyes, half crazed with worry for his little one. If Ellie did nothing, the girl would die. She'd suffocate. Already, the skin surrounding her lips was turning pale.

"I'm going to perform a tracheotomy." Ellie stood up abruptly, and Henry did as well.

"A w-what?" Mr. Thackery stammered.

"Violet's airway is blocked. Most likely her epiglottis—a flap of cartilage that covers the windpipe—is so swollen that it can't open to allow her to suck air into her lungs. A tracheotomy will bypass the swollen epiglottis and give her another way to breathe."

"But how?" Mr. Thackery pressed.

"I'll have to make an incision in her throat and insert a hollow tube."

Henry gripped her by the elbow. He didn't say anything, but the question was in his alarmed gaze. *Had she performed a tracheotomy before?* She hadn't. Nor had she assisted during one. All Ellie knew about the procedure was what she had studied in her medical texts and once observed in the operating theatre.

Violet's father paled. "That sounds...I don't know, doc."

Ellie slipped from Henry's hold on her elbow and went to Mr. Thackery. She took a deep, bracing breath. "I know you're frightened. I am too. But if we sit by and wait, I believe Violet will die. The tracheotomy *is* our last option."

Mrs. Booker grimaced as she held him more firmly. His legs had gone soft, his chin wobbled. He closed his eyes.

"Trust Doctor Ellie," Mrs. Booker whispered in his ear.

Mr. Thackery nodded. "Okay. Okay, doc."

With his permission granted, Ellie's nerves attacked en masse —not that she could show them to anyone else in the room. *Confidence only*, she scolded herself.

She turned to find Henry clearing off the counter and draping it with a length of clean linen.

"Tamora, Mr. Thackery, can you get Violet up here onto the counter?" Ellie asked. "Mrs. Booker, I'll need as much light as possible. And roll up a blanket and place it under the curve of her neck."

The positioning would extend her neck and make accessing the trachea more straightforward.

"What else do you need?" Henry asked as Ellie rolled the sleeves of her shirtwaist to above the elbow.

"I should have most things in my bag, but I don't have a cannula or a dilator." When Henry frowned in confusion, she explained, "I need a hollow tube."

He looked to the apothecary case at the other end of the long counter.

"The syringe we used for the antitoxin," he said. "If we remove the needle and the plunger, the syringe is just a tube."

The thin, one-milliliter size of the tube would be sufficient, neither too large nor too small.

"Is the glass strong?" Ellie asked as he opened the case to retrieve the sterilized needle and syringe.

"It's Siemens glass," he replied. "Compressed and tempered. It's safe."

Again, she trusted him without question.

"We need to wash our hands, quickly," Ellie said, and she and Henry hurried to the kitchen out back.

"Am I assisting you?" he asked as he rolled his sleeves and secured them with the garters. He sounded almost incredulous.

"I'll need help," she answered, scrubbing her fingers and nails and wrists with the bar of carbolic soap she'd brought from the infirmary. She couldn't ignore the slight trembling of her muscles.

She moved aside to let Henry wash at the basin and as he scrubbed, he stole a look in her direction. His eyes betrayed the same apprehension coursing through Ellie. She nearly gave her tongue free rein to blurt how uncertain and inexperienced she was in this kind of surgical procedure.

They rinsed and toweled off, then before she could speak,

Henry took her by the forearms. His grip was firm, his hands warm, and when he met her eyes, her shivering instantly ceased.

"You're a talented doctor. You know what you're doing."

"But I've never done this procedure before," she whispered. Henry shook his head.

"Your training won't fail you. You won't *allow* yourself to fail if I know you at all."

He held on to her, and Ellie had the curious and sudden wish that he wouldn't let go. If they could just stand like this forever, she would always feel safe. But Violet needed her.

"Let's go," she said with a nod, and Henry released her.

They returned to the shop front, where every child and parent was awake and alert and staring apprehensively toward the counter where Tamora, Mr. Thackery, and Mrs. Booker all stood with Violet. The little girl was covered with a blanket from the chest down, and someone had accurately thought to remove her high-necked dress.

The doubt and fear that had just overwhelmed her in the kitchen evaporated like mist when she saw her small patient laid out, waiting for her. Needing her. Violet's breathing was a strident wheeze as Ellie removed her operation kit from her bag.

"Doctor Goodwin, use this to sterilize the glass tube and Violet's throat." She took a bottle of ethanol from her bag and handed it to him. "Tamora, bring the lamps closer to her head."

Tamora repositioned the three lanterns, shedding as much light as Ellie was going to have for the procedure, while Henry cleaned the glass funnel and Ellie prepared the chloroform mask.

The mask was a simple wire and cotton linen contraption that, once ready, she placed over Violet's nose and mouth. She wasn't inhaling very deeply, her throat too constricted, so when Ellie removed the mask and picked up her scalpel, she prayed the anesthesia had taken effect. There was simply no time to wait. The girl's lips and chin were blue, almost bruised from lack of air.

Ellie felt Violet's throat, her fingers identifying the larynx before descending another centimeter to the trachea. From what Ellie could recall from her books, the curved hollow at the very top of the chest, between the collarbones, would be the ideal spot to place a breathing tube.

"I'm making the incision." Ellie took a bracing breath and then made a three-centimeter, vertical incision with the tip of the scalpel.

"Henry, clear the blood," she instructed, dropping his proper form of address without thought. He swiped the trickling of blood, and when Ellie pulled apart the vertical slit, she saw the fibrous column of the trachea.

"I need to make a horizontal incision, between these rings," she announced, mostly to talk herself through it than to inform anyone else who was looking on. Ligaments banded the fibrous trachea cartilage in thick, protruding rings; her scalpel made the incision between two of the cartilage rings.

"Needle nose forceps," she requested as soon as the notch was made. She dropped the scalpel, and Henry placed the forceps into her hand a second later. Ellie widened the slit far enough to place the tube, which she requested next, and which Henry again placed into her waiting palm.

He'd already removed the needle and plunger, as necessary. Cautiously, Ellie inserted one end of the slim tube. She retracted the forceps and immediately, the cartilage snapped closed around the tube, followed quickly by the vertical incision on Violet's neck.

Ellie held her breath. There was no sound for a moment—but then, the rattling of air coming through the placed syringe met her ears. Violet's chest rose and fell as she sucked in greedy gasps.

"It worked," Henry said. A round of exhales and cheers erupted behind Ellie.

She stared at the placed tube, relief coursing through her as the little girl's blue lips flushed pink again. The urge to cry tears of joy was only kept at bay by the knowledge that she wasn't finished quite yet.

"I need to place a few stitches around the tube to hold it in place, and then bandage her neck to keep bacteria from the wound."

Though her fingers were red with blood, Ellie merely wiped her hands on a towel that Tamora handed her before threading her suture needle with black floss thread. The stitches were simple enough, though her attention kept darting to the placed tube. The glass fogged a little with Violet's breath, a sight that kept the sting of tears pricking at Ellie's eyes. She blinked them back, completed the stitches, and bandaged her neck, before facing Mr. Thackery.

Tears wet the man's cheeks as he came to stand at Violet's head. "Doc, I can't thank you enough. You saved my little girl." His hand trembled as he smoothed back her pale hair. Her lashes fluttered a little, but she still slept.

"The chloroform will wear off soon, and when she wakes, we'll have to make sure she keeps her hands away from her neck," Ellie said as a shivering sensation started up in her arms and legs. "As soon as the swelling in her upper throat reduces, we can remove the tube."

Tamora laid a hand on Ellie's shoulder. The weight of it steadied her, and the brief tensing of her fingers expressed warmth. "Go wash up, doc. I'll watch Violet."

She didn't need telling twice. The kitchen all but rushed at her as she hurried toward it.

It had worked. She'd done it. Violet could breathe again. And Ellie could too. She gulped in a few breaths as she plunged her hands into the basin, the blood tinging the water pink as she scrubbed her nails.

The floorboards creaked behind her. A quick look over her shoulder showed Henry, rolling down his sleeves.

"Are you okay?" he asked, his voice hushed and gentle.

Ellie scrubbed harder. "Of course. The procedure was a success, and Violet is breathing."

So then, why was she still shaking?

Henry came to the basin and reached for the bar of carbolic soap in her hand. She'd scrubbed her skin to a bright, painful pink. He set the soap on a dish and captured her damp wrist.

"Ellie."

His voice undid her. Its deep tenor reached into her, obliterating the strength she'd forced into her spine and legs. Her eyes shot to his and in that moment, she gave into the shivers wracking her body. Ellie folded against him, though she didn't know if his arms had come around her first, or if she'd simply fallen against his chest. All she knew was that Henry's arms wrapped around her in a firm, locking hold, and that her cheek was pressed against his chest. She breathed in traces of woodsmoke and musky amber and cedar wood.

A small, alarmed voice screamed from the very back of her mind that she was being absurd. That she was humiliating herself.

"I'm sorry, I..." she murmured. "I don't know what's wrong with me. I'm not upset. I'm happy."

When Henry spoke, the reverberations shuttled through her with astonishing solace. "You just performed surgery on a little girl who was about to die. If you weren't affected, I'd worry you were made of stone instead of flesh and blood."

"But I'm a doctor. It shouldn't affect me this way," she replied, still speaking into his chest. So solid and strong, she noted with ever shrinking decorum.

Ellie pulled back, attempting to infuse some modesty into the moment, even though Henry's embrace felt warm and safe. With another stab of embarrassment, she realized her cheeks were wet. She swiped at the spilled tears, then touched the damp spot on his soft wool vest.

"Goodness, this is humiliating."

Henry covered her fingers, trapping them against the wool. "You're human." He squeezed slightly. "And one hell of a doctor."

Her eyes were hot and teary still when she looked up at him with a reserved grin. "Now you're just trying to make me feel better."

He arched a brow. "Is it working?"

A laugh, husky and trembling, escaped her lips. She sniffled. "A little bit."

Henry's palm slowly slid away from Ellie's hand, though for another protracted moment her palm seemed to stick to his vest, like a thorn clinging onto the wool. She pulled it back and caught a furtive glance from Henry as she fumbled for the towel.

"I should get out there and check on Violet," she said.

He frowned, the expression the polar opposite of the indulgent grin he'd just been wearing. "You need to rest. It's nearly ten o'clock, and Tamora told me you barely slept last night."

"Neither did she," Ellie replied, bristling at being told what to do.

"You're the only one who can perform a tracheotomy if another child needs it," was his sharp—and convincing—reply.

She hung the towel back onto the hook on the side of the basin. "Fine. I will look in on the children, and then try to sleep."

"There's a bed in the back room," Henry said, following Ellie into the shop front. She grimaced.

"It belonged to Frank Eberly." She was about to say that she'd just take one of the cots, but as she looked around, she realized there wasn't a spare, not with the additional children and parents. Ellie prayed more patients didn't arrive overnight.

Violet had been carefully removed from the counter and placed back onto her cot. Tamora nodded reassuringly as Ellie approached.

"She sounds good," the midwife said. "Breathing is strong and steady. Her pulse is normal."

Indeed, when Ellie listened to the child's lungs and heart with her stethoscope, the sighed with satisfaction.

"She's still swollen and feverish, but we can give her another dose of phenacetin in a few hours and hopefully, the swelling will reduce by morning," Ellie told Mr. Thackery. He'd pulled his chair next to Violet's cot and was dabbing her forehead with a cool cloth.

Gratitude brimmed in his eyes. "Thank you, Doctor Ellie. My wife and I'll make sure we find a way to pay you for all this trouble you've gone to."

Ellie flushed. Payment hadn't even crossed her mind. "Oh, Mr. Thackery, no, please don't concern yourself with that right now. My only desire is to see each and every one of these children well again."

She rose quickly before he could argue with her, and after checking on the other children, all of whom seemed to be breathing well and with reduced fevers, exhaustion suddenly settled on her shoulders like a heavy cloak.

There were no extra blankets, so after sterilizing the instruments she'd used earlier and reorganizing her bag, Ellie simply took her heavy wool jacket from the coat stand near the front door and brought it with her into Frank's back room. Myra must have stripped the mattress after his death, for she found the slim bedstead with a bare pallet. The room was chilled several degrees cooler than the main shop with its many bodies and leaping potbelly stove.

With her boots still on, Ellie wrapped herself in her jacket, lay down on the pallet, and propped her head with her tucked arm. She sunk down, out of consciousness, within seconds, her last thought of Henry and his clean scent when he'd held her.

CHAPTER 12

*E*llie ran up Green Street, toward her infirmary. The windows of The Canary were pitch black, and she knew in her heart that something was wrong.

Why would Dade have closed his saloon? Unable to breathe, she pushed open the door to her infirmary and stumbled inside. Frost glistened on every surface. Ellie paused, uncertain and freezing. Unable to remember why she'd come here. But then, her eyes landed on the glass-fronted supply cabinet.

The bottles of medicines had been replaced with rows of bullets. They were lined up neat and orderly behind the glass, but when she opened the cabinet door, bullets overflowed off the narrow shelves, spilling toward the floor. Ellie tried to catch them, but they slipped through her fingers, striking around her feet like loud, banging gunfire. She jumped back, cringing, preparing for a bullet to pierce her.

"Doctor Lennox?"

Ellie's eyes snapped open. Sunlight filled an unfamiliar room. Movement at her side had her sitting up with a gasp, whipping toward the intruder. Only, it wasn't an intruder at all.

Henry Goodwin crouched next to the bed, a frown fixed into place on his lips, as usual. Dread poured into Ellie's chest.

"What time is it?" Her throat was bone dry. Her eyes searched for a clock. "What's happened to Violet?"

"Nothing has happened, she's doing well," he answered. "And it's nearly nine o'clock."

Nine? How could she have slept for so long? Ellie stood up quickly—too quickly. Her head spun as she got to her feet. Henry steadied her, gripping her arm.

"The other children. How are their fevers? Have any more patients arrived?" she asked, trying to force her vision to quit spinning. Hunger gnawed low in her stomach as the glorious scent of eggs wafted from the front of the shop.

"They're all doing well, and there hasn't been anyone since you've been asleep. I promise, everything is fine. Audrey brought breakfast, I thought you might want some." He released her as soon as the room was still again and she wasn't teetering to the side.

She clutched her coat around her, though it wasn't as cold in the back room as it had been the night before. A fire flickered through the grate of the shin-high stove nearby. Someone had built a fire in it overnight. Henry?

"Thank you," she said. "I'm famished."

Why her mind chose that moment to recall him holding her in the kitchen after Violet's tracheotomy, she didn't know. With several solid hours of sleep to fortify her, Ellie found the memory of losing control of her emotions in front of him even more embarrassing than it had been then. Goodness, had she really wept into his vest?

"How are you feeling?" he asked when they had stood in awkward silence for a handful of moments.

"Well. Much better. I was overtired," she said quickly. Before he could comment, Ellie swept from the room into the front of the shop.

As Henry had said, the children were doing well. Sitting up, sipping water, eating eggs, and nibbling on Audrey's biscuits. Ellie went straight to Violet, who was awake, though lying flat on her back.

Mr. Thackery stood as she approached. "Doc, she says she's thirsty, but I don't know if she can sip anything with that tube in her neck."

Ellie sat beside the girl and asked her to open her mouth. Sure enough, as Ellie had suspected, the swelling had reduced overnight. She smiled down at the little girl, who looked terrified. At least she was alert, though, with only a small fever.

"Small sips of water should be fine. Violet, I think you're going to be able to breathe on your own. Let's get a little water and a bite or two of eggs into you, and then I think I should be able to remove the tube."

She looked relieved, as did her father. Her sores were beginning to flake, as were the spots on some of the other children. The worst had come and gone, Ellie knew, and so long as no other ill children arrived today, she started to hope that the quarantine could close in another day or two.

Her muscles quivery with relief, Ellie poured herself a tin mug of coffee and exhaled in relief. Henry stayed on the other side of the counter as she ate a fast breakfast, as if trying to put some distance between them. She tried not to cringe. What must he think of her, breaking down as she had last night? He had seemed to understand then, but in the light of day, maybe he'd come to the realization that professional doctors didn't act in that way.

The thought dragged her stomach low, threatening her tentative happiness.

A quick rapping on the front door to the shop sunk it completely—though, only until Ellie saw that a future patient wasn't standing on the other side of the glass.

She set down her mug and rushed to the door, opening it wide enough to come face to face with Jack.

"You're back," she said, her breath fogging the air. Ellie stepped outside and closed the door behind her.

Jack looked her over, concern etched in the space between his brows. "I heard there was an outbreak of scarlet fever. How is everyone?"

Three-days-worth of stubble covered his chin and cheeks, and Ellie couldn't help but think the rugged look suited him. The worry in his eyes, however, did not.

"The children are all doing well. There was an emergency last night, but…" She didn't want to explain the tracheotomy right now, shivering out front of the shop. What she wanted was to know what Jack had found out in Grantstown from Tom. *If* he'd lived.

Jack stepped closer. "Emergency?"

She shook her head. "It's handled, and everything is fine now," she finished abruptly. *She hoped.* "Tell me what happened with Tom."

He waited a long moment, as if he wasn't ready to let her comment about an emergency go. But then, after a gust of wind shuttled around them, he crossed his arms and turned serious. "He came around long enough to spill on what Hodge is up to."

Hope bubbled, followed by a stab of fear.

"Said a train's coming through, and Hodge plans to rob it."

Ellie fought against the shove of another wind gust. "Myra said their targets were usually trains and banks." So, this really wasn't anything too out of the ordinary for them.

"Chet Hodge isn't known for his ingenuity," Jack said with a wry lift of his brow.

"Which train? When?" she asked.

Frustration thinned his lips. "Apparently, Hodge isn't trusting his own posse with many details."

Thinking of Tom's plan to give Rachel a tell-all story and

confess to Jack for immunity from the law, Ellie murmured, "For good reason, it seems."

Over Jack's shoulder, she spotted Katherine Toft, bundled in a burgundy wool jacket and matching hat, carrying a small wooden crate as she hurried down Main Street toward the shop.

"Whatever's on that train, it's got to be worth something hefty. I'm guessing it's a supply train for a bank," Jack said. "I'll send a telegram to the Colorado Central Railroad headquarters in Denver to see if they have any trains moving through here soon."

It seemed about the only thing he could do at this point. Ellie wished Tom had known more, but at least it was something.

"Were you able to place a telephone call to Sheriff Payton's family in Denver?" she asked.

"Switchboard operator couldn't find them. Said they must not be on the exchange." Jack rubbed his bristled chin. "I suppose I should head back to the ranch, get cleaned up a bit."

Ellie closed her coat around her more tightly, grinning. "I don't know, I think I like it. Very mountain man of you."

A coy smile inched across his mouth, but it flattened out again. "Doc, you aren't in danger of catching this fever, are you?"

She had to admit, she liked the idea of him being a little worried about her. But then felt guilty for it. The last few days, she hadn't given Jack, or his being in Grantstown, a spare thought.

"No, I don't believe so," she said. Unlike Henry, she hadn't had scarlet fever as a child and wouldn't be immune, but she'd been exposed to the illness before, in Boston, and hadn't come down with it.

Katherine reached them then. "Ellie! How is everyone inside? Audrey said little Violet couldn't breathe last night?"

Audrey must have heard the story when she delivered breakfast. She wondered how fast the tale would spread around town.

"I had to perform a tracheotomy, yes, but she's doing well and breathing just fine now." Ellie still had to remove the glass syringe—another first that gave her a tremor of anxiety. Much easier, however, than placing the tube.

The door to the shop opened behind Ellie, and when she spun around, Henry filled the entrance. He saw Katherine and came outside, shutting the door to the quarantine.

"Miss Toft," he said, his tone pitched slightly higher than his usual gruff one.

A wide grin broke out across her face. "Doctor Goodwin, I'd heard you arrived. I'm so glad you could be here to help our dear Doctor Lennox."

Jack hitched his hands on his hips. "You took the train in from Grantstown for the quarantine?" The question of why was plain, even if he didn't voice it specifically.

Henry spared Jack a quick nod, though he shifted his attention back to Katherine. "That's right. I brought an antiserum that was able to help the children."

Ellie watched Katherine struggle to hold the wooden crate in her arms, though she barely seemed to notice the burden she was smiling so brightly at Henry. He reached out for the crate.

"Let me help you with that," he said, and Katherine happily handed it over to him. Ellie bit the inside of her cheek at the young woman's fixed attention on Henry's face. She was utterly smitten with the pharmacist. Something unpleasant curled through Ellie's stomach, but only until she caught sight of something bright orange through the slim gaps in the crate's slats.

"Katherine, are those *oranges*?" Ellie gasped, standing on tip toe to peer inside the top of the open crate.

"Yes! They arrived yesterday. I ordered them for the Christmas dance—you know how wonderful they smell when studded with nutmeg." She caught her breath and still gazing up at Henry, continued, "But I figured the children might like a treat sooner than that."

The idea of the citrus made Ellie's tongue water. In Boston, she would see and eat oranges often, but she hadn't seen one in Sage Canyon at all.

"This is wonderful," she exclaimed. "Thank you for thinking of them."

Katherine blushed. "Oh, it's my pleasure. And I've put another tin of coffee in there and your newspapers," she added.

Ellie had followed Katherine's father's lead and subscribed to a few Eastern papers, including the *Boston Globe* and *New York Post*. They were always a week or two old when they arrived at the mercantile, but she didn't mind. It was just nice reading about what was happening on the other side of the country. It was so easy to forget the rest of the world even existed, being way out here, pinned between two mountains at the base of the Rockies.

"Doctor Goodwin, do you think I could speak to you for a moment?" Katherine asked, and by the furtive glance she took at Ellie and Jack, it was clear she wanted to speak to Henry alone.

"Of course." He took Katherine aside, walking far enough away so that their voices were mere murmurs.

"Wonder what that's all about," Jack muttered.

Ellie turned away from them, forcing another odd curl in the pit of her stomach to straighten out. "I'm just glad you're back," she said, and added hastily, "and that Tom survived. You have something to go on now."

It seemed like ages ago that she had been in Grantstown with Jack, meeting with Rachel and then coming upon the horribly injured ex-Hodge gang member. Ages ago since she'd been brooding over the fact that he didn't have the same feelings for her that she did for him.

"I heard Nate Walker's taken off," Jack said. His mind had been moving along a totally different tangent. A non-romantic one. Clearing her head, she nodded.

"That's right," Ellie said. "Myra's staying at McClure's."

"And he didn't tell her where he went." He sounded skeptical.

"He thinks it's safer for Myra and the baby if he stays away right now, until everything with Chet Hodge clears up."

Jack crossed his arms. "Or maybe he's gone to meet up with Hodge after all."

Disappointed, Ellie crossed her arms as well. "You don't believe that."

"It's awfully convenient," he replied.

Cold had creeped up through the soles of her boots. She knew better than to argue with Jack when he was being stubborn. Deep down, he didn't believe Nate had gone back to Hodge. He *couldn't* believe it. He and Myra were starting fresh; they were starting a *family*.

Though, Ellie had to admit that Nate's disappearance could easily be interpreted in the way Jack had suggested. And he and Myra would need a way to support themselves and their child. Nate had been doing odd jobs around town, but nothing steady. People here were hesitant to trust him. People like Jack.

"I need to get back inside," Ellie said. It was true, but it was also a way to escape the turn in the conversation.

Jack caught her arm when she turned for the door. "Hey."

Warmth flashed up on her wrist, where he held her. The prickling sensation lingered until she gently pulled out of his grip.

"I want to believe in him," he said, holding her gaze. "Everyone deserves a second chance."

She parted her lips, then sealed them. He was only talking about Nate Walker...wasn't he? Not about their broken romance, cut off at the knees before it could even truly begin?

A smile wobbled to her lips. Jack tugged the brim of his Stetson and then turned out into the street, making his way past Henry and Katherine, who were still in huddled conversation. Ellie avoided Henry's glance in her direction, though she saw it from the corner of her vision. She fled inside the warm shop—her cheeks already burning.

CHAPTER 13

The edge of tension that had subdued the scarlet fever quarantine started to dull by that evening. No new patients had arrived, and the children who had been ill were turning a corner, making their way toward recovery. Even Violet, whose tracheotomy removal had gone smoothly, was doing well. And Graham Booker still showed no sign of having contracted the illness. It was a huge relief for both Mrs. Booker and Ellie, whose chest loosened, bit by bit, from the clench of worry with every passing hour.

The temperature in the shop dropped as evening came on, bringing with it the steady whistling of wind. Henry was diligent about feeding the stoves in the front and back rooms, but frost still built on the corners of the windowpanes. Conversation between Henry and Ellie had been stunted throughout the day, each of them too busy for anything more than a few words here and there. For her part, Ellie knew she was purposefully avoiding him. The night before, when he'd held her, kept creeping back into her mind, as did the twinge of envy when she thought of his and Katherine's hushed conversation that morning.

She gritted her teeth and shook her head. This was absurd.

The close quarters had gotten to her. What she really needed was some fresh air and an escape from quarantine. The chance to stretch her legs and be alone was so tempting, she could feel the muscles in her calves tensing, ready for the chance to move.

The arrival of Audrey and Maggie and baskets of food for supper, gave Ellie's twitchy nerves a moment of reprieve. Grateful, she opened the door to accept the baskets and sucked in a lungful of fresh, crisp air. It had a peculiar scent to it, one that Ellie recognized. Snow was coming.

"Thank you so much," Ellie said, handing the baskets to Tamora and Mrs. Booker. "We're indebted to you for taking care of us."

Audrey had sent Caleb over at lunch, and Mrs. Thackery, too, had delivered a few hot loaves of bread and a small crock of butter for the children. Staying in quarantine had been a trial, but Ellie had to admit, they had been well-fed the entire time.

"Not at all. We take care of each other around here." Audrey leaned close and whispered, "Meet me at the back door." Without waiting for Ellie's reply, she gave Maggie a parting wave and headed toward the exterior corner of the shop.

"How are the Bookers?" Maggie asked, looking over Ellie's shoulder. She had tutored the boys from time to time.

"Bobby is doing well, and Graham has stayed healthy all along."

Relief relaxed Maggie's expression. "I'm so glad. Tell them I'll visit as soon as they get home."

Ellie nodded and was about to close the door when Maggie exclaimed, "Oh! I forgot to tell you. Fiona had her baby!"

Ellie flung the door open again. "Did she? How is she? And the baby?"

"They're both just fine. It was a boy, and they've named him Sean. That was our pa's name," she said.

Even with the cold air sneaking under her collar, Ellie warmed at the good news. After bidding Maggie goodbye, she ducked back inside and hurried to the back room. As she went to the door, she thought of how she'd found it the night of Frank's murder: open wide, snow drifting inside. Ellie felt a little guilty for having suspected Myra, even just a little, when she'd looked at her dead father's body with such loathing. It was now clear the shooting had been linked to Chet Hodge and, as Jack had discovered, his plan to rob a train. He must have come to recruit Nate again, and instead, met with Frank.

Ellie unlocked the door and found Audrey on the other side. She hurried in, extending a smaller basket covered with a cloth.

"What's this?" Ellie asked, closing the door.

"I thought you might want to eat alone," she replied, then with a mischievous grin, added, "And selfishly, I missed you. It's been days! How are you?"

Ellie tried to look chastising. "I missed you too, but this is a quarantine."

"I don't see any children in here," Audrey said defiantly as she took off her jacket.

Ellie sighed. "Oh, all right. But I'm only giving in because I missed you too, and I want to hear about everything that's been going on while we've been stuck in here."

They pulled chairs closer to the stove, and Ellie dug into the food Audrey had sorted into a basket just for her: sweet rolls, spiced ham, perfectly cooked carrots, and a slice of butter cake that made her want to get to dessert quickly.

"Fiona had her baby," Audrey said.

Mouth full of sweet roll, Ellie replied, "Maggie told me. A healthy boy." The words were muffled by food, which only made the two of them laugh. Once Ellie swallowed the bite, she tried again. "Will you and Maggie take the train to Grantstown to visit?"

"As soon as this quarantine closes up," Audrey replied.

"Thank goodness. We'd starve."

Audrey shook her head, chuckling. "Oh, I haven't been doing

it on my own. Did you know that people keep coming by with things for me cook for you and the children? Carrots, yams, onions, a whole ham," she said, gesturing toward the forkful of ham Ellie had just put in her mouth. "Word's gotten around town about what you did for Violet too. I wouldn't be surprised if even Mayor Carson and Muriel changed their minds about you."

Ellie nearly choked on a laugh. She didn't see that happening anytime soon, but she was hopeful that public opinion of her might be shifting.

"I won't hold my breath," she replied, wiping the corner of her lips with the napkin Audrey had tucked into the basket. She always seemed to think of everything. How blessed Ellie had been to be taken in by such a caring woman. What she'd said, about how people take care of each other in Sage Canyon, was true—and Audrey more so than anyone else.

"I heard Katherine delivered oranges for the children."

"We devoured them earlier, and Tamora squeezed a few to make juice." Charlie and Lucy had turned up their noses at the peeled fruit, making Ellie wish she'd thought to bring her jar of peppermint sticks from the infirmary. After all the bitter willow bark and slippery elm tea they'd been consuming, the children deserved a treat.

"I saved the peels for you," Ellie added as she ate some more ham and carrots. "Tamora said you can make tea from dried rinds."

Audrey looked pleased by that. "I'm glad she's here with you."

The midwife and Ellie had started off on the wrong foot months ago, but now, it was clear she and Tamora simply had two different sets of skills and knowledge—and they complemented each other nicely.

"So am I. She's been invaluable."

Audrey shifted in her seat. "And Doctor Goodwin too, I imagine."

The bite of sweet roll felt coarse and dry all the sudden. Ellie nodded, forcing the mouthful down. "The antitoxin made a difference."

"I was surprised when he joined the quarantine," Audrey went on. "He could have delivered the medicine and returned to Grantstown."

She was fishing around for something. Some tidbits of information about why Henry had sacrificed days and days to stay. The question had also lingered in the back of Ellie's mind.

"He wanted to observe its effects," Ellie said blandly. Audrey's forehead crinkled and flashed her a look that said, *Oh, really?*

Before she could say anything verbally, though, Ellie set her plate on the top of the stove and stood up. "Katherine also brought me my newspapers," she said, thankful for the diversion. The papers were still in the crate, which she had set on the bed. She hadn't had a moment to look through them, but now, figured it would be something to distract Audrey from her leading questions about Henry.

The *Globe* and *New York Post* were both several days old, but news from outside Sage Canyon and Grantstown, even a bit dated, was still welcome. She handed Audrey the *Post* and sat down in her chair with the *Globe*. The broadsides had met with a little dampness on their way west and the ink had run in spots.

"Look at these prices for shirtwaists," Audrey huffed, having bypassed the front page for the inner pages, where the advertisements were placed. "A dollar for soft batiste. They're twice as expensive in Grantstown!"

Ellie had noticed the increased cost of goods in the west too. However, it wasn't the advertisements drawing her attention at the moment. She'd opened to the second page of the *Globe* and while reading the blotted headlines, tripped to a halt on one in particular.

Child Dies of Morphine Overdose. Doctor Stands Accused.

Ellie's lungs turned to stone as she blinked at the large, bold headline. Then, ears ringing, she read the first paragraphs of the article.

"Ellie?" Audrey's voice sounded muffled under the pounding of blood in Ellie's ears. "What's wrong?"

"I…this article, it's…oh my goodness." She'd rushed so quickly over the words that she had to go back and start again. Though her voice trembled, she read aloud:

"Doctor Stanley Hargrove, renowned physician at Children's Hospital, has been temporarily suspended from duties after a girl has died under his care. The child, Emily Parker, 9, had recently emerged from a successful operation to remove an enlarged abscess of the throat. Doctor Hargrove stands accused of administering an excessive and deadly amount of morphine to treat the child's post-operative pain. Hargrove faces a legal inquisition and investigation…"

Ellie's throat closed off. She could read aloud no more. She and Audrey sat in silence for a moment, the logs in the stove crackling.

Then, Audrey said, "You've mentioned that name before. Hargrove."

Ellie nodded, gooseflesh riddling her skin. "Yes. He's the physician I assisted. I worked under him, he was my mentor, and…"

And it was Doctor Hargrove who had tasked Ellie with giving Todd Andrews a dose of morphine that fateful night last summer. Doctor Hargrove had been in a rush to leave the hospital, to get home to a dinner party or some other event, and he'd known Ellie would stay the night. The ward had been filled with fever patients, and Ellie had been working non-stop for days. Todd wasn't her patient; he wasn't even sick with the yellow fever numerous other patients had been admitted for. Doctor Hargrove had removed Todd's appendix that afternoon.

She related this to Audrey, whose eyes narrowed with every

word. Her lips were pressed together, and lines formed between her brows.

"Ellie, you've told me before that you don't remember giving Todd that morphine injection."

It was true. She didn't remember, but she had been over-worked. Exhausted. She did recall seeing Todd in his hospital bed; he'd been sleeping peacefully. But the chart had shown a morphine injection had been administered and Ellie had initialed it.

"I don't know what to make of this article," Ellie said after a few moments. She folded the paper, knowing she would go back to it when she could get her thoughts straight. "Doctor Hargrove is one of the most respected physicians at the hospital. In *Boston*."

"Do you not believe he's to blame?" Audrey asked.

"No. He can't be," she answered, but even as she said it, doubt trickled in.

Audrey rested a hand on Ellie's, which she realized she'd balled into a fist on her lap.

"All doctors make mistakes," she said softly.

"Yes, but this same mistake? It seems…" Ellie didn't know how to finish. Anything was possible. She'd made a glaring mistake, and a boy had paid for it with his life. The guilt and fault lay solely with her.

But now, Doctor Hargrove stood accused of the same form of malpractice. Morphine overdose. Was it merely a coincidence? She'd never been one to accept coincidences easily, but this *must* be one.

Audrey checked the date on the *Globe*. "This over a week old. Nearly two. Much more has happened since it printed. Why don't you write to your sister?"

The mention of writing a letter jogged loose the memory of receiving Matthew's letter. Somehow, she'd forgotten all about it. The business with Chet Hodge and now the quarantine had shoved its importance into the far back of her mind. She'd have to check the date of his letter, but it seemed possible that he'd written to her *after* Doctor Hargrove was accused.

Her stomach cinched at the connection she'd drawn. Was that why Matthew had written? He hadn't said anything about Doctor Hargrove, but surely, being right there in Boston, he had to have heard about it.

Ellie folded the paper and set it on the floor. She then rubbed at her eyes. She was too tired, too worn down to think of it right then.

"I'll write to Pearl," she belatedly replied to Audrey. She stood. "I should get back out there and check on the children."

Audrey sighed, as if she knew she was being dismissed, and got to her feet. But she was too stubborn to let Ellie off the hook too easily. "Don't let that article get under your skin right now. You can deal with whatever it means later."

As usual, she was right. There were more pressing matters to attend to right then.

"Thank you for supper," she said, giving Audrey an embrace. In that moment, she longed for her room at McClure's. The warm, comfortable bed, the blazing stove, the familiar ticking of the clock that usually lulled her to sleep at night.

"If everything goes well the next two days, we'll be able to close the quarantine and send the children home," she told Audrey.

She gave Ellie an extra squeeze before stepping back and picking up her jacket. "It will be good to have you back at McClure's. I don't know if I can take another moment of Caleb and Maggie's flirtatious glances. I've caught them kissing twice!"

Ellie laughed. "I don't know how my presence will stop any of that."

"Oh, it won't," she said, opening the back door. "But at least I'll have someone to groan about it with."

Audrey winked before closing the door. Ellie wasn't fooled for a moment; she knew Audrey adored Maggie. However, seeing her only child falling in love, and knowing how shy and special Caleb was, must have been worrisome for Audrey. She wouldn't want Caleb's heart broken. Maggie was a fine young woman, but Ellie knew too well how hurtful changes of heart could be.

Her throat ached a little, thinking of Jack. Of Matthew too, she supposed. It was odd how she'd been ready to marry Matthew, and yet his severing of their relationship had hurt less than Jack's decision that he wasn't yet ready to begin a relationship.

She shook her head to clear it and went into the front of the shop. Children and parents were all finishing up their meals, and Henry and Tamora were seated at the counter, near the cash till, with their plates.

"Where've you been?" Henry asked, looking Ellie over with a concerned glance.

"Eating with Audrey," she explained, and at his chastising eyebrow arch, waved her hand. "Oh, it was just for a few minutes."

Tamora set her empty plate on the counter. "I'll squeeze a few more of those oranges. The children said their throats felt better after sipping the juice."

Ellie grimaced, remembering the peeled rinds she had wrapped in a linen kerchief and placed inside her jacket pocket to give to Audrey. Ah well. She'd just have to give them to her later.

Once Tamora had walked away, Ellie and Henry remained, awkwardly silent. Fed up and feeling absurd, she broke the silence. "I expect we can close the quarantine in another day or two."

"Excellent."

"I'm sure you're ready to return home," she added, thinking of her own recent longing for her room at McClure's.

Henry stood up and collected Tamora's empty plate. "I have something to see to here in town before I take the train back."

Ellie parted her lips, then closed them. "I see."

It had to do with Katherine Toft, she presumed, and their earlier conversation. Not that it was any of her business. Or interest. Suddenly, she couldn't stand still another moment. An idea popped into her head; an excuse to flee the quarantine, if only for a few minutes.

"I'm going to the infirmary," she said, walking around the corner of the counter and toward the coat stand near the door. Henry followed.

"Do you need something that isn't in your bag?"

She threw her coat on and buttoned it to the neck. "Just some peppermint sticks." At his confused look, she added, "For the children."

"I can walk with you," he said. Ellie tied her scarf too tightly around her neck.

"Oh, no, that's not necessary. I'll be just a few minutes. It's right across the street."

And then, before she could even finish pulling on her hat, a lady's brown felt fedora, she swept out the door and closed it firmly behind her. She exhaled, her breaths clouding in the twilight.

The abrupt exit had been inelegant but she didn't care. As soon as she started moving toward Green Street, Ellie felt better, as if strings that had been binding her had been snipped free. She put all thoughts of Doctor Hargrove and Henry Goodwin and Katherine Toft and Jack Granger aside and lengthened her stride. The Canary was bustling, as usual, unlike like her eerie dream just before waking that morning, where the saloon had been dark and silent, and her infirmary, layered in frost.

Unlocking the door, Ellie stepped into the cold, dark infirmary. She drew up short at the frosty air. A hot snap of unease went down the back of her neck as she thought of her dream again. But it was absurd. The frosty air made sense, considering she hadn't been here the few days to light the stove. *It was just a dream.*

The glass canister of peppermint sticks sat on her desk, and as she walked to it, she pushed away the apprehension crawling up her back. Instead, she busied her mind by thinking of other things she could do to prolong her visit at the infirmary. *Other* than knock on the saloon door and engage Dade in conversation.

But really, there was nothing for it. She didn't need anything but the canister. Heaving a sigh, she picked it up—then went still at a sound in the shadowed corner of the infirmary. The door leading to the backyard, where there was a small square of grass, an outhouse, and a well pump, opened. The hinges squealed and the small hairs on Ellie's arms stood on end.

The open door let in some of the deep blue twilight, which was now inky shadow. A figure slipped inside the infirmary. A man. Ellie's heart seized. "Who's there?" she called.

The man came closer, and with a surge of relief, she recognized him. The tension in her shoulders released. "Sheriff Payton! My goodness, you gave me a fright."

What on earth was he doing here? And entering the infirmary through the back door, too.

"You're back from Denver already?"

He ignored her question. "I need you to come with me."

"Is someone ill?" Her pulse ratcheted up again. "Has there been an accident?"

Payton hesitated before answering. "An accident, yes."

There was something odd about how he said it, but Ellie brushed it aside. She set the canister of peppermint sticks back onto the edge of the desk. "My doctor's bag is at the quarantine. I'll get it, and then we can—"

Sheriff Payton drew his revolver from his hip belt and leveled it at her. "Can't do that, doc. Just grab what you need from here and let's go."

CHAPTER 14

*E*llie stared at the weapon in the sheriff's hand. "W-what are you doing?"

He jerked the silver barrel of the revolver. "I don't have time to give you answers. Hurry up."

A shiver of panic stroked through her as she made her way toward the supply cabinets, her dumbfounded stare still on his gun. Ellie's hip hit the side of the desk; the glass canister rattled and dropped off the edge, smashing onto the floor. Peppermint sticks and glass shards scattered all around her feet. Sheriff Payton hissed, his eyes jumping to the connecting door to the saloon.

"Dammit, doc, if anyone comes in here, you'll leave me no choice. Hurry up and be quiet about it," he said.

Next door, piano music and muted conversation continued on. No one had heard the jar shattering. Ellie, her mind racing, pulled a smaller satchel from a wall peg, one she usually carried with her to Toft's to hold cans and other items. With shaking arms, she collected an assortment of supplies.

"What kind of injury is it?" she asked.

"A gash. Deep one. Looks infected." Payton kept the gun

trained on her. He shifted, as if agitated. What in the world was he doing? He was the town's *sheriff* for goodness's sake! Jack had mentored him. Trusted him.

Ellie finished gathering some things she might need and shouldered the bag. "Sheriff, I don't know what's happening, but if you're in trouble—"

"Shut up. Get over here." He jerked the gun again and with a gasping breath, she slunk toward him, stunned by his behavior.

He grabbed her arm. "Don't even think about shouting or making a run for it."

Fear drove into her. This wasn't the sheriff she knew. He'd always been courteous, if a little stiff and by-the-books. Jack had thought so too and had even seemed bothered by how Payton followed the rule of law so strictly.

He jostled her through the back door, down a rickety set of wooden steps, into the small yard behind the infirmary. A saddled horse waited next to the outhouse.

"Where are we going?" Ellie asked.

"I said shut up," he whispered, and yanked her arm to move faster.

A burst of laughter and a short, cracking sound came from The Canary. Ellie twisted her head and saw a woman in an upstairs window. She'd just shut the window and now moved out of sight. Ellie's heart sank. The woman was one of Dade's workers. If only she'd caught a glimpse of Ellie being dragged away. How was anyone going to know where she'd been taken? And how long until Henry or Tamora became curious about why she was taking so long at the infirmary? They would arrive to find a smashed peppermints jar and nothing else. They might find footprints out back, in the snow. Would it be enough? Could they track the horse's prints?

With a flare of inspiration, Ellie remembered the orange peels in her coat pocket. She reached in as deftly as she could in the moments before Sheriff Payton reached his horse. Her fingers felt the bundle of peels in the kerchief; she fished around, gripped a peel with shaking fingers, and flicked it out, onto the snow. She prayed Payton didn't spot it.

"Mount up," he ordered, shoving her toward the horse.

Ellie fumbled a little as she got into the saddle, but within seconds, Payton mounted behind her, clicked his tongue, and they trotted off, quick. At least he hadn't noticed the peel. Then again, no one else might, either. Still, short of screaming and making a commotion—something that might end with her getting a bullet lodged in her back—the peels were all Ellie had. There had to be dozens of them in her pocket, all in varying sizes. The children had enjoyed peeling the oranges almost as much as they'd enjoyed eating them. *The children.*

"Please, sheriff, I'm needed at the quarantine. There are sick children—"

"From what I hear they're doing fine. This can't wait."

His arms closed around Ellie as he gripped the reins. As Payton took them on a course away from the town's buildings, toward the base of West Mountain, the motion was rough and jarring. He cut south and headed for the train tracks. It seemed as though he was trying to keep out of sight from any homes and buildings. To her right, Ellie saw lamplight dotting the row of miner's homes, though they quickly cantered by them, toward a stretch of darkness. The only thing ahead was empty scrubland and forested hills.

"Who is injured?" Ellie asked as she reached into her pocket again for another couple of peels. She dropped them, trying not to move her arm noticeably.

Payton didn't reply for a few moments, and Ellie feared he'd seen her drop the peels. She waited, heart pounding as the horse shuttled them across a stretch of flat scrubland, covered in snow. The moonlight was dim, hidden as it was behind pockets of thick clouds.

"Chet Hodge," the sheriff finally answered. Ellie sucked in a gulp of air and twisted in the saddle to stare up at him.

"You're working for Chet Hodge? But you're the sheriff!"

He gave his horse another flick of the reins and they rode faster. When he said nothing, Ellie added, "How could you? That man's gang killed Jack's wife."

"Listen, I never intended for any of this to happen," he finally said. "I didn't have a choice."

"What happened?" she asked, even though no matter what he said, no matter what his excuse, he had still crossed the line of the law.

"My brother got into a bad scrape in Denver a while back. That's where Chet's been the last few years," he said as he led the horse into a line of trees. They seemed to be heading eastward, in the general direction of Grantstown.

Ellie dropped another peel of orange, hoping she wasn't spreading them out too far and wide.

"Rick owed Chet money. A lot of money," he went on. "Chet came to me and offered a deal. I help him out, and he lets Rick off the hook."

Disappointment settled, heavy in her chest. Sheriff Payton had kneeled to a threat made by a criminal to protect his brother. "You could have asked your friends for help," she said. "The people of Sage Canyon trusted you. If you'd only—"

"I won't gamble with my brother's life," he snapped.

The horse, feeling its rider's tension, trotted faster. Ellie tossed down another couple of peels.

"You're helping Hodge with the train robbery," she said.

Payton scoffed. "Old Tom blabbed to Granger after all, I see."

"At least he was trying to do the right thing."

"He just wanted a fat payout for his story and immunity from prosecution. Tom's no angel."

The sheriff was probably right about that, but Ellie still felt sickened.

"How are you helping Hodge?" she asked.

"I was a sharpshooter in the army," he replied, surprising her with his direct answer. "Chet needs someone on a bluff when the train comes through the pass."

Ellie's stomach clenched. "You're going to shoot someone?"

He tightened his hold, pinning Ellie's arm. Her hand was in her pocket, closed around a few more peels. Now, she couldn't move to toss them down.

"No more talking," he grunted.

She wiggled. "You're hurting me." It wasn't true, but she needed him to loosen his arm. It had been too long since she'd dropped another clue for anyone who came to track her. *If anyone tries at all.*

Reluctantly, Payton accommodated her.

"You never went to Denver, did you?" she asked. "Your father didn't die."

"I said no more talking."

She used the distraction of his flaring temper to let another couple peels go.

"You've carried me off into the night, against my will, Sheriff Payton. I have a right to know why."

"Uppity woman," he hissed. "You've got no rights, not anymore. The only thing you need to know is that Chet's hurt, and you'd better be able to fix him."

She clenched her jaw as they rode deeper into the hills. The cold air had numbed her cheeks and her kneecaps, too. Thank goodness she was wearing her thicker winter boots, scarf, and hat. Her ungloved fingers, however, were nearly frozen. They fumbled with the peels as she furtively dropped them every other minute or so.

"Say I can manage to help Hodge," she said after a little while. "What then?"

He didn't answer. A different kind of chill seeped into her at his silence. Ellie wanted to believe that Payton would bring her back to Sage Canyon. That he'd let her go. But she knew too much now. If he planned to "return from Denver" after the train robbery, she couldn't be there to call him out as crooked.

"You just worry about helping Chet for right now," he finally replied.

He wasn't going to let her go.

Dread filled her as they wound deeper along the path through the hills; it was single track and narrow but trampled. Meaning if someone followed her trail of rinds, they might also find this track.

She drew out another handful of peels, but before she could toss them, Payton went rigid in the saddle.

"What's that smell?"

Ellie breathed in and knew what he'd scented: orange citrus.

He wrenched her hand up and the peels scattered into her lap. Payton let out a coarse growl and swore as he dug into her coat pocket and found the rest of the peels. He dumped them all into the snow, and then, using his leather gloved hand, pinched her chin between his thumb and fingers roughly.

"You best hope no one follows that bread crumb trail you've been leaving." His fingers bore into her skin, and this time, he *was* hurting her. "Anyone who comes after you isn't going to walk away. You got that?"

He let go of her chin and slapped the reins. They rode onward, the trail of orange peels ending. Regret burned through her, stealing away the cold. If anyone did come for her, if they managed to find her at all, they would be in grave danger. Goodness, what if it was Henry? He didn't even have a gun. She hoped he would be wise and seek out Deputy Munns and Jack. Or at least Tamora, who did own a rifle.

The horse's hooves crunched along the snowy path, the moon gliding out from behind clouds every so often. Ellie's ears were frozen, her teeth chattering, her ribs aching from Payton's tightened arms, when at long last, the warm glow of light appeared

through the trees. A small shack, no bigger or better than a dilap-
idated woodshed, stood in a small clearing. A shadow holding a
long rifle peeled off one tree.

"Who goes there?" a deep voice called.

The sheriff slowed his horse. "It's Payton. I've got the doctor."

The man lowered his rifle. "Hurry up. He's in a bad way."

Payton dismounted, and then all but dragged Ellie from the
saddle. She landed in the snow, staggering to the side with sharp
pain shooting through her frozen feet. Indignant, she shook off
his grip.

"I can't help him if I'm injured myself," she snapped.

The shadow whistled. "Got a whip of a tongue, don't she?" He
sounded amused, rather than angry. But Payton only grabbed
hold of her arm again and hustled her forward, toward the shack.

He shoved open the door and flung Ellie forward, into the
smoky confines of the shack. At least it was warm. A wrought
iron stove piped out heat, and a few lanterns gave off light. One
man stood at the stove, another sat in a chair, and a third man
reclined in a cot, shaking under a thin blanket. The reclining
man's skin glistened with sweat. Feverish, wracked with chills—it
had to be Chet Hodge. He lowered the gun he'd pointed at the
door out of caution.

"Bring her here," he grunted, heaving himself up onto an
elbow.

Payton nudged Ellie. "You heard him. Go."

She approached the cot warily. Every beat of her heart
thudded in her chest with more effort than usual. "Mr. Hodge,"
she said, her throat parched. "I was told you have a wound."

And by the poor look of him, it was probably infected.

"Damn right, I do." He brought his bandaged hand up for her
to see. The wrapping was soiled with grime and perhaps dried
blood. Ellie stifled an admonishment that keeping the wound
clean would have been in his best interest.

"I'm going to have to look at it." She dragged a cane-backed chair with a ripped wicker seat over and sat down, careful not to send her bottom through the frayed hole in the seat. She set her satchel on the floor at her feet.

The foul smell of unwashed clothes and body odor assaulted her nose as she nimbly took his hand and began unwrapping the poor excuse of a bandage. The fabric was stiff with dirt and blood, and when she finally unraveled it, letting it fall to the floor, another odor struck her nostrils: the rancid smell of rot.

She pinched off her next breath and fought the sick climbing her throat. The man's hand had a long, deep gash straight through the palm, and the torn flesh was black and oozing.

"Mr. Hodge," she began, gritting her molars. "What caused this?"

"Knife," he grunted. "One of my men came at me with it. Thought he could get rid of me and take over."

"You teached him, Chet," the man standing next to the stove put in.

"Hank got what was coming to him, the traitor," the seated man added.

Ellie frowned. "Hank Jerrick? That's why you killed him?"

Chet Hodge lifted his glassy eyes and curled his lip, which was hidden behind a wealth of scraggly whiskers. "You here to question me or fix my hand?"

She hitched her chin and redirected her attention to the gash. Among the supplies she'd hurriedly stuffed into her satchel was a bottle of ethanol, though even as she poured it over his palm and tried to clean the wound as thoroughly as possible, she knew it was far too late to prevent infection. Hodge's teeth were chattering, his skin was pale and clammy, and he was breathing rapidly.

"Get me a drink, Marcus," Hodge grumbled, and the seated man leaped up to bring him a cup. Hodge drank greedily.

"Have you been very thirsty?" Ellie asked, her stomach souring with a sinking suspicion.

"Can't seem to quench it," he answered, water glistening on his beard.

"Are you feeling dizzy and nauseous?"

"Yeah. So? Stitch me up already."

Ellie exhaled, calculating the days since the gash had been inflicted. It had been nearly a week since she and Tamora had found Hank Jerrick with a bullet in his head.

Trepidation filled her as she realized the extent of Hodge's infection.

"Mr. Hodge, I can clean and stitch your wound and put on a new bandage, but…" She gathered a breath, hoping for courage. "The infection has entered your blood stream. These symptoms —dizziness, nausea, extreme thirst—they point to low blood pressure. In addition to your high fever, the shakes you're experiencing…I'm afraid that I must diagnose a case of sepsis shock."

Hodge narrowed his eyes at her. "What in hell is that?"

Ellie considered how best to explain. "It occurs when bacteria enter the body through a wound such as this. Often, a person's body can fight the bacteria, but other times, it takes hold and… well, it can't be fought."

The truth was it wasn't entirely known why some people could fight the pathogens that introduced disease and other people could not. Proper wound care, washing one's hands, and keeping surgical tools sterilized were some ways physicians were learning to stem the occurrence. But this wound had clearly not been treated well.

Hodge snatched his hand back, out of her hold. With his uninjured hand, he again gripped his pistol and aimed it at her. "I brought you here to fix me up."

Though her pulse stuttered at the pointed gun, Ellie sat firm. "I won't lie to you, Mr. Hodge, whether you aim that weapon at me or not. As a doctor, I have a responsibility to be truthful, even when the truth is dire. There is no cure for sepsis shock."

His nostrils flared. Booted feet scraped the floor behind Ellie, but she refused to tear her glare away from Hodge's. A hand clapped down onto her shoulder.

"You heard the man. Stitch him up."

Ellie shrugged out from under Payton's heavy hand. She'd brought a suturing kit and without another word, got to work. Stitching the wound would not matter in the end. Sepsis shock was rarely survivable. Right then, Chet Hodge's organs were failing him. It could be hours, or a few days, before he died. There was no way to tell.

As soon as she finished the sutures, she unrolled the linen wrap she'd brought and made a few passes over his hand, knotting it off tightly. He tucked his hand up against his side.

"You got anything you can give me for this sepsis thing you say I've got?" he asked.

She held still, trying not to shrink from his steely glare. "No. There is nothing. Not here or in any physician's office."

He clicked back the hammer on his pistol. The sound locked up Ellie's lungs and throat.

"Then I 'spose there's nothing else I need you for."

CHAPTER 15

*T*he cabin went silent. Or maybe Ellie's ears had only muffled with panic. She held her breath, waiting for the shot. Waiting for the pain. Several seconds that felt like an eternity went by, and Hodge still hadn't pulled the trigger.

"You ain't gonna beg for your life?" he asked.

"I don't see how it would help," Ellie replied.

Hodge's scowl broke, twisting up into a sneering kind of grin. "Sure won't. But on second thought, killing a doctor might be shortsighted of me. You might come in handy after tomorrow's raid."

Cautiously hopeful, her pulse lunged forward like a racehorse breaking free of the opening gate. Hodge let his gun rest on the cot beside him. He reset the hammer, and she fought the urge to cry out with relief.

"Raid?" she repeated, breathless as her heart attempted to resume its normal rhythm.

He didn't respond, but as he laid back down and shut his eyes, Ellie figured he was referring to the train robbery Jack had learned about. It was happening tomorrow?

She packed up her satchel and stole a look at her watch fob, strung on a gold chain on her vest. It was nearly one in the morning. She'd been gone for hours. Her stomach cinched at the thought of the children back at Eberly's. Ellie would never have abandoned them; they had to know that. Surely, Henry and Tamora and the other parents knew something had happened to her.

Payton took her by the shoulder again, urging her up and out of the chair.

"Stay over there," he ordered, pointing to a corner of the cabin, behind Hodge.

Ellie regretted moving away from the stove as she followed the sheriff's terse order and retreated to the corner. There was no chair for her to sit upon, and so after a few moments of standing on what felt like two blocks of ice for feet, she lowered herself to the dingy floor and stretched her booted heels as close to the stove as she could. The bare board floor was only a few degrees warmer than the snowy ground outside, she reckoned, but she couldn't complain—she was still alive, wasn't she?

But for how long?

On top of Hodge's internal organs deteriorating, his mind would also begin to slow and malfunction. Sepsis patients were known to be crazed or hallucinate as their brains were consumed by the disease. Hodge could very well change his mind and order her shot.

Ellie couldn't contain her shivers as she tried to dissolve into the shadowy corner. The men's eyes flicked toward her every now and then, and another concerning worry arose. These men were *not* gentlemen. They weren't decent in the least. Men like these wouldn't think anything of harming a woman. Even the sheriff might turn a blind eye if it meant staying in Hodge's good graces.

She had a scalpel in her satchel but no other weapon. And really what could a small scalpel blade do against a gun?

But thankfully, none of the men did more than cast her

furtive, curious looks over the next few hours. Ellie nodded off a few times, her lids heavy, her eyes burning with exhaustion. But she would snap awake quickly, afraid sleeping would only leave her more vulnerable. She also wondered if somewhere out there, her orange peel trail had been discovered. A rescue came with its risks, of course. She didn't want anyone she cared about in danger, but she also knew that Hodge wasn't going to let her go willingly.

Hodge himself continued to rest uneasily, his shivering increasing as dawn neared. The cot in which he laid rattled from his uncontrollable shaking. The windows, though grimy, brightened with the rising sun. A few times, Hodge called out as if having a nightmare. His men were attentive, if apprehensive, and Ellie wondered if they had come around to believing what she'd said about sepsis being incurable. Were they considering what they would do if their leader died? With the raid happening that day, would Hodge even be fit to take part?

Her backside was numb and aching when finally, the man named Marcus cautiously shook Hodge's shoulder to wake him. He tossed up his hands in surrender as Hodge jerked awake and aimed his gun.

"Just me, boss. It's morning. You said we should get going at dawn."

Hodge lowered his weapon and struggled to sit up. When Marcus tried to help, Hodge swiped at him and swore. "I can get up myself. I ain't no invalid."

He staggered to the side as he stood. His eyes cut to Ellie, who also stood and felt the ache of it after she'd sat so long on the hard floor.

"Coffee," Hodge ordered, and another man rushed forward with a tin mug. Payton leaned against the wall near the front door, his arms crossed in indifference.

Hodge sipped the coffee but spit it out. Growling with impatience, he waved his hand toward the door.

"Clear out," he barked. As Marcus and the other man grabbed their things and headed outside, Hodge stopped in front of Payton.

"Tie her up and make sure she don't get loose. Then get yourself to the bluff over the pass."

Without sparing Ellie another look, Hodge left the cabin. Payton shifted his jaw, visibly irritated at needing to take orders from the man.

"I need to relieve myself," Ellie said to him once they were alone. Her cheeks warmed at admitting such a personal need, but it couldn't be helped, especially if he planned to tie her up.

Payton jerked his gun at the door. "Outside then," he muttered.

Did he have no shame over his choices? He acted irritated, as if put out by all this outlaw business. And to think, she'd thought him respectable. He'd fooled everyone. As she walked into the bleak morning sunlight, she thought of how the people in Sage Canyon would react if they knew how low their sheriff had fallen. And Jack... If he ever found out, he'd be stunned and furious. That's why Ellie didn't believe Payton or Hodge were going to let her go.

The trees were a mix of pines and spruces, and aspens and maples. Winter had stripped the aspens and maples of their leaves, but the forest was still thick with green boughs from the conifers. Boot prints marred the snow around the shed, which looked even more decrepit by the light of day.

"Over there." Payton gestured with his weapon toward a thin line of stunted pines. Ellie started for them when he added, "And don't try to run."

He didn't need to explain what would happen if she did. Only an irrational ninny would try to make a run for it. She was in the middle of the Rocky Mountains, somewhere between Sage Canyon and Grantstown. And the sheriff had already admitted to being a sharpshooter.

However, as she crouched behind the shrubs with hope that Payton held no interest in spying on her, she wondered what she *could* do to escape. Reasoning with the man seemed the only option.

"Sheriff," she said, as she emerged a few minutes later, "please listen to logic. You're a lawman, respected and trusted, and if you explain your predicament, why you felt you had no other choice but to help Hodge, I'm certain that you'd—"

"Shut your mouth. Get back into the cabin." His terse, emotionless words chilled her. Despondent, Ellie took heavy-limbed steps back toward the cabin. The open door waited. Somehow, she knew if she went inside, she wouldn't be coming out again.

She went still. "No."

"What did you say?"

Ellie had never bowed down to a man before, not while she'd been in school, not when she'd been practicing in Boston, and not here, in Colorado. She'd always known, right from the start, that bowing down once would lead to twice, and then a third time, and from there, the dominos would continue to collapse.

"I said no." She turned and looked Payton in the eye. "If you're going to shoot me, then do it now. Or let me go."

When push came to shove, killing an unarmed woman might not sit well with him. Then again, his desperation might be so severe, his conscience so weak, that he would think nothing of it.

Payton scowled. "You don't seem to understand, doc. I'm not the one in charge here. Chet Hodge is. I thought you were smart enough to know that."

He raised his pistol, the thin barrel pointed right at her. Ellie lost feeling in her body, though blood rushed through her ears in a furor.

And then, another man's voice broke through the snowy clearing. "I've got the back of your skull right in my crosshairs, Payton. Drop your gun."

Ellie sucked in a breath as the sheriff stiffened. Nate Walker emerged from behind a thick-trunked fir tree about twenty paces away.

"Walker," Payton grunted. Ellie's legs felt like jam preserves but she locked her knees and stayed upright.

"Do as I say," Nate warned.

Fury beaded the sheriff's eyes, but he lowered his gun and tossed it aside, well out of reach.

"Doc, find me some rope," Nate then said, and with her gummy knees, she rushed into the shed.

Her heart thumped wildly as she found a length of rope hanging from a nail and hurried back outside with it. Nate had come closer, his gun still trained on the sheriff.

"Hold your hands behind your back," Nate ordered, his tone as unflinching and serious as the steady aim of his gun. "The doc's going tie you up. If you move, I won't hesitate to shoot. I've got no qualms killing crooked lawmen."

The sheriff shook his head and after a reluctant moment, stuck his hands behind his back and put his wrists together. Approaching him felt dangerous, but she did as Nate said, wrapping Payton's wrists with the rope and then, as tightly as she could, made a knot.

"Get on the ground, ankles together," Nate ordered next.

"Walker, you sonofa—"

"Don't make the mistake of thinking I won't put a bullet into you the same way you did Frank."

Shock poured through Ellie, and she nearly stumbled. "*You* shot Frank Eberly?"

Payton dropped to his knees and then onto his side.

"Bring the loose end of the rope down to his ankles and tie them," Nate instructed, and as Ellie crouched to do just that, he explained, "I didn't tend to listen to Frank when he was sober, let alone when he was drunk, but that night Frank had come back from The Canary mumbling something about the sheriff still being in town. You heard Dade saying the same thing, doc. How he thought the sheriff wanted to put him in jail for something."

She did recall Dade mentioning it now. "You knew he'd seen you," she whispered to the sheriff.

"And you needed to shut him up," Nate tacked on.

With newly trembling hands—this time fueled by anger—Ellie cinched the rope tight around Payton's ankles. He lay on the snow, trussed up like a farm animal, his jaw clenched.

"He was an old fool," he spat. "Wasn't a loss to no one, and you know it, Walker. The man was worthless."

"That didn't give you the right to kill him," Ellie said.

The sheriff had shown up at Frank's back door, and Frank had let him in without hesitation, without fear. He'd been shot in cold blood by someone he knew and trusted. Somehow, that made his murder even more wretched.

Ellie backed away from him, now understanding why reasoning with Payton to let her go would never have worked. He'd crossed too many lines when it came to the law; there was no way out for him now. Payton avoided looking at either of them as she crunched through the snow toward Nate.

"Thank you, Mr. Walker," she said, her voice tremulous. "How did you know where to find me?"

The notion that he'd discovered the orange peel trail cleared when he explained that he'd been in these woods for a few days, ever since leaving town. He'd spotted one of Chet's men and trailed him, laying low to observe the cabin and their comings and goings.

"I figured out their target for the raid yesterday and was just about to head back into Sage Canyon when I saw Payton here bringing you into the cabin. I knew Chet was injured, and I knew it was a risk leaving you in that cabin overnight, but my one gun against the Hodge boys wouldn't be enough," he said. "It was safer to wait until morning to have a clear shot."

Ellie nodded, understanding.

"You aren't...hurt, are you?" Nate asked, lowering his voice, and hesitating over the words just long enough for her to comprehend what he meant.

"No, I'm all right," she assured him. "But Chet Hodge isn't. He's developed sepsis and won't likely make it through the next few days. Not that it's going to stop him from raiding that train. When is it coming through?"

If there was time to get back to Sage Canyon and alert Jack and Munns, or even the authorities in Grantstown, they might be able to stop the robbery. But Nate quashed that possibility.

"Less than an hour," he replied. "It's a money train. They're planning to blow the track and send the whole thing off the rails. Payton here was going to pick off the engineer and guards if any survived the wreck."

Ellie nodded, recalling Chet's instruction for the sheriff to get to the bluff as soon as she'd been tied up. "Is there any way to stop them from blowing up the track?"

Nate shifted his jaw and nodded, slowly. "I think there might be if I can get to that bluff. But we'll have to ride fast." He glanced toward the sheriff's horse, still saddled and roped off on a low hanging tree limb. "You know how to ride?"

"Don't you dare take my horse," Payton growled from where he lay on the ground.

"Don't worry, sheriff, you won't be needing him in prison," Ellie said as she untied the horse and mounted. She soothed the nervous animal with a few gentle strokes of her hand when he recognized a different rider.

"I left my mount out of sight. Follow me," Nate said, heading back into the woodland.

"You can't just leave me here on the ground, Walker!"

Ellie followed Nate, neither of them responding to the sheriff's cries as they left. Sorrow filled her heart, but not for Payton's predicament. His choices had been his own, and now he'd have to live with them.

The only thing that mattered now was making it to the bluff before Hodge's gang derailed that money train.

CHAPTER 16

*I*t didn't take long for Payton's horse to settle after they picked up Nate's mount and started toward the bluff. All the while, astonishment over her changed fate kept Ellie reeling. One moment, death had been certain; the next, she'd been awarded another chance at life. She nearly felt giddy with wonder. A sense of urgency wound her muscles tightly, too—not just to reach the bluff and stop Hodge, but also to make something of this second chance. Surely, it had been granted to her for a good reason. The children in the quarantine entered her mind first. Yes, she'd saved some lives, but she'd also been the reason for one boy's death.

Again, the newspaper article she and Audrey read the evening before—though now, it seemed like weeks ago—sowed doubt on the events surrounding Todd's death. It was nothing to dwell on, however, not as they were wending their way up a rocky path, hooves slipping here and there on loose stones and dirt.

At last, Nate held up his hand. Then touched his index finger to his lips, indicating the need for silence. As their horses ascended onto a flat clearing, distant voices reached Ellie's ears. She and Nate dismounted, roping off their mounts on bare, snow-topped aspen limbs. The sun had broken through a banking of clouds, and snowflakes glittered in blinding winks and flashes as Nate and Ellie edged toward the bluff's overlook.

Nate had taken the long rifle from the sheriff's saddle earlier and now dropped, belly down onto the snow while gripping it. Ellie lowered herself to the ground too. Cold bit through the wool of her skirt as she elbowed her way forward.

"There," Nate said softly.

Down a steep slope studded with boulders, scrub pines, and a few lanky-trunked spruces, a section of train track curved into sight and ran straight through a logged clearing for a couple hundred yards. The Hodge gang worked near the steel rails, unaware of Nate and Ellie's arrival.

"Move back," Nate whispered. "If anyone looks up, they'll just think I'm Payton getting into position."

Ellie scuttled in reverse, losing her view of the train track and the gang. She frowned and whispered, "I only counted three men."

"I don't see Chet," Nate said.

Ellie scanned the rocky bluff behind her, uneasy at the gang leader's absence. None of the horses had been visible below. It was possible Hodge was hanging back with the mounts. He might have even lost consciousness. The simple act of riding could have been enough to incapacitate someone in his condition.

All was silent except for the sporadic muttering and grunting coming from the tracks. Then came the distant blare of a train whistle. Ellie stiffened. Nate, sprawled on the ground, tucked the rifle into his shoulder, cocked his head, and squinted through the crosshairs.

"They're setting the explosives," he told her in a hushed tone.

"The train is coming," she said, needlessly. He'd heard its whistle just as well as she had. "What are you going to do?"

He didn't answer, and she supposed he didn't need to. He wasn't holding the rifle for no reason.

"Must you kill them?" she asked.

"They aren't good men, doc."

"You were once one of them, and *you're* a good man," she reminded him.

He let out a long breath. "It's them or the people on that train."

Innocent people would die if it went off the rails. Ellie couldn't let that happen, not if they could prevent it.

"Do what you have to," she said, though a knot had formed in her throat.

"Get ready," he warned. A second later, the rifle went off, sending up a trail of smoke. Instantly, pandemonium broke out below.

"One's down, but the other two are coming this way," Nate said.

Fear clawed up her back, but then, another gunshot echoed. More shouting erupted.

"What the—" Nate lowered the rifle and lifted himself higher onto his elbows to stare over the bluff. Ellie could take it no longer—she crawled back to the edge to see what was happening.

A tangle of men swarmed the base of the hill, clashing with the two Hodge gang members left standing. One particularly dark Stetson hat caught Ellie's eye.

"It's Jack!" she cried.

He leveled his gun at one of the Hodge boys and shouted for him to put up his hands. Her heart swelled. Jack had found her. Either that, or he'd simply discovered where and when the raid was going to happen.

Two other men, Deputy Munns and Dade by the looks of it, rounded up the other man.

A *click* behind Ellie sent the hairs on the back of her neck on end. Nate went rigid beside her.

"Traitor scum."

Chet Hodge. Only now did Ellie hear his laborious breathing, the crunch of his boots on the snow. The commotion below had masked his approach.

Slowly, still on the ground with the cold seeping through her skirts, Ellie turned. Hodge stood a few yards away, his blotchy skin bathed in sweat. His uninjured hand shook. He barely looked able to lift the weapon high enough to aim at Nate.

"You'd rather shoot me than make a run for it?" Nate asked.

Firing his weapon would alert Jack and the others. Hodge might be able to then mount his horse and take off, but in his deteriorating condition, it didn't look like he'd make it far.

"Doc here says I'm done for anyhow," he wheezed. His lips were so dry, they'd cracked. Blood speckled his whiskered chin. "Got nothing to lose."

Regretfully, he was right. That strangely giddy sensation at having a second chance at life evaporated like mountain mist. He had his gun on them and nothing but desperation fueling him. Vengeance was likely important to a man like Hodge.

"You believe me now?" she asked him, hoping to buy some time, keep him talking—though to what end? Jack might not even know she and Nate were on the bluff, or that Hodge had found them.

"I can feel it." He coughed and shuddered; the fever had likely become dangerously high.

"Don't make murder the last thing you do," she replied.

He only rasped with laughter. "First, second, or last, it don't matter."

A motion behind Hodge drew Ellie's attention, and a man appeared. Heat flooded her, followed by fathomless dread. It pulled her heart so low she thought she might be ill.

It was *Henry*.

"Lower your gun." His deep baritone seemed to vibrate within Ellie's chest. He cocked the hammer on the revolver in his hand, and Hodge hitched his chin. Where in the world had Henry gotten that?

"I don't know you," Hodge replied without looking over his shoulder.

"Introductions aren't necessary," Henry said. "Throw your gun to the side."

Henry gripped his revolver naturally, his arm relaxed, and his expression dangerously serious. Ellie couldn't blink, couldn't breathe. If Chet Hodge spun around, he might shoot—and he was likely a very good marksman.

Fear spiraled through her at the image of Henry, shot, bleeding on the snow. He shouldn't be here. He shouldn't have ever come to Sage Canyon. He could have sent the antitoxin on the train and left it at that. Why had he insisted on staying? On searching for her out here in the wilderness?

"Shoot him, Goodwin," Nate said, still motionless on the ground next to Ellie.

"You shut up," Hodge grunted.

"Why? You're a dead man anyway," Nate pestered.

"Mr. Hodge," Ellie began. "There is still a chance the sepsis won't kill you. A small one, but it's not impossible. If you were to give up your weapon and let us take you back to Sage Canyon—"

"Grantstown is closer," Henry cut in. Ellie met his eyes. He nodded slightly, as if realizing what she was trying to do.

"Grantstown, then," she amended.

Indecision crossed Hodge's face, and in an instant, Ellie knew he did not want to die. He hadn't given up, not yet. Criminal though he was, she would uphold her word and try to get him treatment.

A chesty cough wracked Hodge's body, and then, unceremoniously, his arm fell slack to his side. With a flick of his wrist, his weapon dropped onto the ground. Nate swung the long rifle around and held Hodge at the end of it as he scrambled to his feet.

Henry lowered his revolver. Ellie wanted to move too but felt frozen to the snow.

"Ellie?" Henry started toward her, his frown deepening. "Ellie, are you hurt?"

As if released from some stupor, she staggered to her feet and launched herself into his arms. He closed them around her in a firm embrace, hanging onto her so tightly she could have let the muscles in her legs go limp. A part of her wanted to. She'd never felt so safe or relieved in her life, though she had felt something similar—when he'd held her during her breakdown after Violet's tracheotomy. Maybe, she thought as his warmth seeped into her, it was just *Henry* who made her feel this way. Ellie breathed in deeply, slightly frightened. Not just of her realization, but at how acutely comforting his arms were. How undeniably strong and reassuring.

"I found the broken jar of peppermint sticks in the infirmary and knew something had happened," he said.

The peppermint sticks. She gasped and pulled back, searching his face. "The children! How are they? Did anyone else come to the quarantine after I'd been taken?"

His lips twitched, hinting at an amused grin, and she frowned. "What?" she asked.

"The children are fine. If you hadn't noticed, *you* were the one in danger."

"Well, yes, but—"

"But you care about the children. I know." Henry touched her cheek, but only briefly. He drew his hand back and again asked, "Are you hurt?"

She shook her head. A lump in her throat prevented her from speaking. He rubbed his hands along her arms as though he wanted to warm her up. Although, she considered he also might have just wanted to keep holding her in some way.

"We found the orange rinds." He arched a brow. "That was smart."

Ellie pretended not to be heartened by his praise, but she

suddenly understood something: She hadn't dropped the rinds for just anyone. She'd left the trail for him.

Again, Henry touched her cheek. This time, however, he didn't pull away. With a gentle nudge of his thumb, Ellie's chin lifted. His attention drifted toward her mouth. Instinctively, she parted her lips, all too aware of how closely they were standing. Of *his* mouth. And how much she wanted to kiss it.

A signaling whistle split the air. Ellie leaped, the small bubble that had formed around her and Henry bursting. With astonishment, she saw Hodge had seated himself on a boulder, looking weakened beyond measure. Nate, still holding the rifle level with the outlaw, waved to the men below. "Up here!" he shouted.

Ellie stepped back, away from Henry, and he did the same while clearing his throat.

"Where did you get that gun?" she asked just as he asked, "Who took you from the infirmary?"

Henry seemed to remember then that he had a revolver in a hip holster. His fingers brushed over the black handle. There was something familiar about that gun.

"Dade loaned it to me. Jack wouldn't let me ride out with his posse unless I had a gun, and well, Dade offered it up."

Its familiarity made sense now. Dade had insisted Ellie carry the same revolver in September, when the Cameron's son was lost, and she and Caleb were joining the search party on West Mountain. The image of Henry not taking no for an answer when it came to riding out to search for Ellie, pushed a smile onto her lips.

"Do you even know how to fire it?" she asked.

"I'm not a complete tenderfoot," he said, defensively. Behind them, Hodge snorted and swore under his breath, no doubt realizing he'd been had by a novice gunslinger.

"When are we heading to Grantstown?" he grunted, still pale and sweaty.

"Who says you're going there?"

Jack had crested the bald-faced bluff, his gun already fixed on Hodge. He flicked his eyes toward Ellie. "Doc, are you okay?"

She nodded, a strange curl of guilt threading down her throat. "I promised him we'd go to Grantstown and seek medical help—"

Jack cocked his gun. "He just might need it."

"No, Jack!" Ellie sprang forward to step in front of him, but Henry caught her arm and hauled her back. She wrenched her arm free. "He has sepsis."

"What's that?" Jack asked, his steely eyed gaze still locked on his old enemy. The man he'd hunted for so long.

"An infection in his blood. It's shutting down his organs and his chances are low, but no matter what he's done, he agreed to lay down his gun in exchange for medical help."

She dragged in a breath, the air snapping with cold. Jack's eyes were just as frosty.

"He killed my wife."

Silence blanketed them. The ferocity in his voice had nearly matched the anguish. His wife's murder had driven him on a course of revenge that had ruined him in more ways than one.

Ellie grappled for what to say, how to convince him to lower his weapon.

"You got no way of knowing if it were my bullet, Granger." Hodge sounded defiant, but the look in his eyes told another story. He believed Jack was going to pull the trigger. His nostrils flared, preparing for it.

Jack repositioned his aim and gritted his teeth. "She would still be alive if you hadn't brought your gang into town. For that, the blame rests on you."

"He's unarmed, Jack," Nate said in a placating tone.

But Jack's fervent glare didn't flinch. "So was Sarah."

In his mind, he was justified. Ellie ached for him, a part of her understanding and even willing to just let him fulfill the craving he'd had since he'd been forced to bury his wife. But even though he'd pulled away from Ellie recently, she still sensed that he wasn't the sort of man who would rest easy killing an unarmed man.

"Jack," she said softly. "You're better than this."

He shook his head once. Shifted his jaw.

"I didn't know Sarah, but I can't believe she would want you to do this."

Hodge was sick. Dying. Yes, a bullet would end him sooner, swifter. But in her heart, Ellie knew—and she was willing to bet Jack knew, too—that it wasn't for him to decide when or how Hodge met his maker.

"If you're not going to shoot him, we should get moving toward Grantstown," Henry said after a few protracted moments. Ellie glared, horrified by his blithe attitude. He only shrugged.

After a long exhale, Jack growled and lowered his gun. Hodge's tensed shoulders dropped.

"Walker," Jack bit off. "Munns and Dade are with the other prisoners. See Ellie safely back to Sage Canyon."

"We got Payton tied up back at Hodge's hideout," Nate supplied. "We'll swing by and grab him."

Jack pulled up short and scowled at Nate. *Payton?* He stared at Ellie next, a mask of confusion twisting his usually handsome features.

"I'm sorry, Jack," she said, wishing he didn't have to feel this disappointment too. "He was working with Hodge. And…he confessed to Frank Eberly's murder."

Blood drained from Jack's face. He turned away before she could see any other reaction, though his head shook back and forth as if he couldn't believe what he'd just heard.

But then, he gestured toward Henry. "Goodwin, you and I will take Hodge to the doctor in Grantstown."

Henry met Ellie's eyes, and a string low in her stomach gave a decisive yank. Jack and Henry urged Hodge to his feet and started leading him down the hill. Confusion wriggled uncomfortably within her. For so long, it had been *Jack* she had wanted to kiss. When he'd started avoiding her, giving her reasons to second guess his affections, she'd felt it as a loss.

Now, however, as she saddled Payton's horse and watched Henry start back for Grantstown, it was a strangely similar loss, and just as keen and puzzling.

CHAPTER 17

A new glass jar filled with peppermint sticks appeared on Ellie's infirmary desk the day after her return to Sage Canyon.

The long, cold ride back to town with Deputy Munns, Nate Walker, and Dade escorting the last two Hodge gang members as well as the disgraced and shackled Sheriff Payton, had been met with such a commotion along Main Street that Audrey had been drawn out of McClure's. She'd nearly sobbed with relief as Ellie had dismounted and fell into her waiting arms.

A hot meal, a warm change of clothes, and endless reassurances that the children in the quarantine were all recovering well and getting ready to return to their own homes had preceded a solid twelve hours of sleep. She had never been so exhausted in her life.

At dawn the following morning, Ellie lay in bed staring at the ceiling for only a few moments, ruminating on how Jack and Henry might have made out in Grantstown, before leaping up and getting dressed. She had work to see to, and letting her mind linger for too long on either Jack or Henry would not benefit her in the least.

At Frank Eberly's shop, she found Tamora holding down the quarantine without any trouble at all. Mrs. Booker and her boys were still there, as were Violet and Mr. Thackery, but the others had all departed. Fevers gone, swelling reduced, and the scarlet rashes entering the final stage of dry, flaky skin, Tamora had conceded that the contagious phase had passed. Perhaps it was because she was still so tired, or because she'd nearly lost her life twice in the previous twenty-four hours, but even though Ellie didn't entirely agree that sending the children home was prudent, she didn't argue. She only embraced Tamora—who stiffened in surprise—and then thanked her.

With a foreign twist of her stomach, Ellie had gathered up Henry's case, which he'd left at the shop. While carrying it to her infirmary, a ridiculously juvenile thought popped into her head— that Henry's hand had gripped the leather handles in the past. Holding them made her feel closer to him. Instant mortification made her blush as she charged down Green Street toward the covered porch steps that fronted the conjoined saloon and infirmary.

It wasn't until she entered the small office that she remembered what had happened when she'd last been there. But the shattered glass jar had been swept up, the peppermints discarded, and with a near overwhelming rush of gratitude, Ellie stared at the new jar of peppermints with hot, teary eyes.

"Katherine Toft brought that over."

Ellie startled, having thought herself alone. But of course, the door to the saloon was open, and Dade was slouched against the doorjamb. His old dog trotted in on his heels.

She swiped at a tear that had escaped. "That was thoughtful of her." She sniffed, setting down the case and removing her jacket.

"I took a peppermint," Dade confessed. "Hope you don't mind."

Ellie laughed as she hung her jacket on the stand. "Mind?

Dade, you deserve all the peppermints you want for helping to find me."

He shifted uncomfortably. "Well, now, let's not go hog wild, doc. I couldn't pass up the chance to join a posse and be a hero, and all."

"Of course," she said with a roll of her eyes. "In that case, you've reached your one peppermint limit. Keep your sticky fingers to yourself."

He snorted a laugh as Ellie checked the back door. A flare of nerves fired up her spine as she recalled Sheriff Payton slipping inside and holding her at the end of his gun.

"Ivy saw you out back with the sheriff," Dade said, having followed the direction of her eyes.

Ellie recalled the figure in the window, closing the sash. "I'd hoped whoever it was noticed me and said something to someone. But it seemed far-fetched."

Dade crouched to rub behind his dog's ears. "When Ivy tried telling Granger she saw you with Payton, he didn't believe her. Said she had to be mistaken."

Ellie couldn't blame him—it had been dark, and the sheriff was supposed to have been in Denver. The fact that Munns and Jack hadn't been able to reach him with a telegram or through the telephone exchange made sense now.

"He fooled everyone," she said, lifting Henry's case and setting it onto her desk. *D.H. Goodwin* had been pressed onto a small brass plate near the handles.

"Only Goodwin listened to her," Dade went on. "He went out back and found them orange peels."

Her heart thudded as she bit her bottom lip and brushed her index finger along the brass plate. "Did he?"

"Yup. Shoot, I thought he was gonna level Granger when he refused to let him ride out with us."

She really shouldn't have been taking so much pleasure in hearing how Henry had reacted to her disappearance. And yet,

Ellie indulged. She also recalled how tightly he'd held her when they'd been on that bluff; the way his eyes had dropped to her lips. If not for Nate's whistle, signaling everyone below, Henry might have kissed her. And she would have welcomed it.

She blinked and cleared her throat. "You lent him the same gun you lent me," she said, hoping to refocus. Dade shrugged.

"The more men on the trail the better. Anyway, I'm glad you're okay, doc. Norma is too," he said with a wink before giving his dog one last scratch and standing up.

"Oh, and don't forget—rent's due," he tacked on before heading back into the saloon.

Ellie's grin faded as she shook her head, crossed the room, and closed the door behind him. She supposed it was back to life, as usual.

For the next half hour or so, Ellie worked between building a fire in the stove to warm the infirmary and making numerous notes on the quarantine and its patients, as well as the administration of the antitoxin serum and its various results. The writings, she knew, were just for her own records, however she couldn't help but consider the possibility that they might be of interest to other physicians. Perhaps even to the *New England Journal of Medicine*. Then again, she doubted the journal would ever publish a doctor with a tarnished reputation.

Ellie tapped her pen on the paper at her elbow, thinking back to the newspaper article about Doctor Hargrove. Every time she thought of it, more questions about Todd Andrews's death wove their way into her mind. *Had* Doctor Hargrove already dosed him with morphine? Had he overlooked it and mistakenly tasked Ellie with dosing him again? There was really no way to know, unless Doctor Hargrove confessed—which was something he wasn't likely to do.

With another sinking feeling in her stomach, she also remembered the letter from Matthew, folded away in her desk drawer back at McClure's. She'd read through it a few times, and his language had continued to bewilder her. Writing about how he'd been wrong to end things, that he knew she might no longer share his feelings, but had to at least try to reach out to her, and then signing it with '*My continued affection,*' had all hinted—strongly—that he had changed his mind about ending their engagement. That he might even want her back.

Ellie glanced at Henry's case on the corner of her desk. Perhaps if he'd written within the first few weeks of her time in Sage Canyon…or if he'd come to the train station in Boston and begged her not to leave… Perhaps then she would have felt differently. But now, the thought of Matthew didn't set off a single spark in her chest. She'd been putting off a reply, but now knew what she had to do.

Pulling forward a clean sheet of paper, Ellie let out a long sigh and wrote:

Dear Matthew,

I was surprised to receive your letter, but I want to thank you for taking the time to write and apologize for our cool parting last summer. At the time, I was angry and confused. I felt you had abandoned me at a time I needed you most and when so many things in my life were in a state of upheaval. However, now, viewing it from a distance, I know I must thank you. I'm currently sitting in my little infirmary in a silver ore mining town on the edge of the Rocky Mountains, where I have found both patients and friends.

Though it is a world away from Boston, I'm happy in Colorado. There is something wild about this place. It is exhilarating and challenging, and while it is also somewhat frightening, I can't imagine being anywhere else.

This is all to say that I hold no resentment or hard feelings toward you, Matthew, but neither do I hold you in the same affection as I once did. I wish you the best and will rest easier knowing we have parted on more pleasant terms.

Your friend, always,

Ellie

. . .

FEELING a weight lift from her shoulders, Ellie blew on the paper to dry the ink. He had been correct in his letter that she didn't appreciate flowery language. Getting straight to the point of what needed to be said was more her style. Matthew would understand her brief but direct reply. Their romance had been steady and smooth, unhindered by tempers and disagreements. Ellie shook her head in incredulity as she grasped, much too late, that their romance had not been in the least bit romantic. Never had she looked into Matthew's eyes and wanted to kiss him desperately; never had she also wanted to scream at him in frustration or fall to pieces in his arms or feel breathless and yet bursting with some unnamed emotion that came alive right in the center of her chest.

These things she had experienced since coming to Sage Canyon. First with Jack, and now... But it was absurd. Yes, Henry had softened toward her since their initial exasperating encounters, but did he truly care for her? The way he'd let her come apart in his arms after Violet's tracheotomy, and his reaction when finding her on that bluff had seemed to indicate it. What then about Katherine Toft? There was clearly something between them.

The swirl of disappointment clipped her wandering thoughts, and Ellie folded the letter to Matthew. She'd post it right away and be done with it. With the stove's fire just barely starting to take hold and warm the infirmary, Ellie, restless, got up to take down her jacket. However, through the window, she spotted Mrs. Booker climbing the porch steps. Ellie's heart stuttered, and she whipped open the front door.

"Is it Bobby? One of the other children?" she inquired, her mind racing toward any possible complications that could have arisen in the hour since she'd left Eberly's shop.

Mrs. Booker shook her head, a grin forming. "They're all just fine."

Ellie exhaled and moved back into the warmth of the infirmary, Mrs. Booker shivering as she followed. "I haven't been outside in days," she exclaimed, rubbing her arms. "Didn't miss it."

"I think I'm still cold from my ordeal in the woods with the Hodge gang," Ellie replied, trying to make light of the dangerous mess she'd been forced into. But Mrs. Booker only shook her head and scowled.

"I can't believe the sheriff went corrupt. I would've sworn on my mother's Bible that man was a good one."

Ellie had heard the same comments from Audrey and Maggie and Myra, all of whom had plied her with hot food, tea, and warm blankets the previous afternoon when she'd returned with the posse. Myra, especially, had been struck dumb by the truth. Though she'd been overjoyed to have Nate back safely, she'd blinked back tears of pain and anger when Nate revealed it was Payton who'd shot Frank, and why.

"Marshal Bevins is supposed to arrive today to take him into custody," Ellie said.

What would happen to him next, she couldn't bear to think about right then. He'd killed a man in cold blood. He'd abducted her. If Nate hadn't come to her rescue when he had, he probably would have killed Ellie too. Like Hodge and his men, Payton's punishment would be justified.

Munns was sure to be promoted to sheriff once the governor received the news about Payton too. Hopefully then, Sage Canyon would start to heal from the breach of trust.

Mrs. Booker reached into her skirt pocket and pulled out a kerchief, bundled around something and knotted at the top. The singing of coins tore Ellie's mind from Munns and Payton entirely, and she blinked at the bundle.

"We took up a collection," Mrs. Booker said. "It isn't much, but what you did for our children is something we can't ever really repay after all."

She held the filled kerchief out to Ellie.

"Oh, Mrs. Booker, this…this isn't…"

The last time she tried to refuse Mrs. Booker's payment, she'd been met with stony-faced insult. Now, she arched an eyebrow and tucked her chin. "Doctor Ellie, you are our town's physician, and this is how we show you how much you are valued."

She picked up Ellie's hand and placed the coin-filled kerchief in her palm.

"And please, call me Mary," she added.

Accepting the money the other parents had collected might have made her squirm with mixed sentiment—she had treated the children to her best ability to save their lives, with no thought at all to payment—but hearing Mrs. Booker ask her to address her as a friend buoyed Ellie's heart.

She closed her hand around the kerchief and nodded, smiling. "Very well, Mary. Thank you."

Mary caught her hand again, and with a significant, steady gaze, said, "Thank *you*, doctor."

She gathered herself up then and opened the door. "Oh, I forgot to ask," she said turning back to Ellie. "Bobby and Graham were wondering if you'll be at the Christmas dance this Saturday? I believe they're planning a surprise for you." Mary's eyes glittered with mischief, and Ellie cocked her head, pleasantly suspicious.

"Is that so? Well, to be honest, I hadn't really given the dance much thought, but now I certainly can't miss it," she said with a laugh.

"You don't want to disappoint your admirers," Mary teased, and with a wave, stepped outside.

Ellie bit her lips, amused and curious at what the two young Booker gentleman might have in store for her. Passing the bundle of coins from one palm to the next, she considered dropping by the bank on her way to the post office. A muffled bark from the other side of the saloon door gave her another idea.

She crossed the room and opened the door, finding Dade behind his bar, watering down the liquor bottles. He held up his hands in surrender.

"It's for the good of the town," he told her. Ellie rolled her eyes and tossed him the kerchief, which he caught deftly. "What's this?"

"Rent," she said, and then closed the door behind her.

CHAPTER 18

"*A*re you *sure* it's not too much?" Ellie asked. She gripped the railing along the stairs at McClure's and stopped on the middle step.

Audrey had weathered the same question gracefully the previous nine times as they were getting ready for the Christmas dance, but the tenth time broke her saintly patience.

She glared at Ellie from where she stood at the bottom of the staircase. "Very well, do you want to hear the truth?"

Ellie's heart plummeted. She'd known the dress was too fancy. Why she had even bothered to pack it was beyond her. In Boston, the Worth evening gown would have been considered standard wear for a holiday party. The dark maroon silk satin with velvet appliqués of deep emerald holly, a half-wrap bodice topped with emerald netting, and capped sleeves trimmed with maroon beaded fringe, had been Ellie's holiday dress the previous year. When she'd lovingly folded the gown and placed it into her trunk bound for Colorado, she'd assumed there might be an occasion for which to wear it again. It wasn't as though anyone would know she'd worn it before. However, after arriving in Sage Canyon, she'd put the elaborate and far-too-fussy gown from her mind almost immediately. It had hung in her closet behind her more practical clothes ever since.

Ellie pursed her lips and nodded. "I'll go change." She would simply put on one of her nicest, everyday dresses and be done with it.

"Don't you dare!" Audrey cried.

Ellie froze, startled at the vehemence in her tone. Audrey came up onto the bottom step and gripped the newel post. "Elliot Lennox, the truth is that you look absolutely gorgeous in that gown, and yes, you will outshine every other woman at the dance, and I could not be happier for it. I want to see the look on Muriel Carson's face when she sees you, and if you don't give me that one small pleasure in life, I will never forgive you."

Ellie covered her mouth with one of her satin-gloved hands and all but giggled.

Audrey beamed up at her and held out her hand. "Now, we are already late, so if you don't mind?"

She continued down the steps, her feet more appropriately clad in a pair of black leather boots. The Worth gown's hem was long enough to conceal all but the tips, and no matter how horrid of a fashion faux pas it was, she couldn't bring herself to walk to the church in the pair of satin heels dyed to the same maroon color. Her feet would have been sore blocks of ice by the time she arrived.

Ellie took Audrey's hand, and her friend giddily tucked her in close to her side. They had spent the last hour in Ellie's room, applying what little cosmetics she'd packed as well. A few strokes of blush, some lip color, and crushed shell powder to give their skin a dewy, moonlit look. Audrey had made faces at herself in the mirror, exclaiming that she was far too old for any of this nonsense, but Ellie had insisted and was now glad she had. Audrey was strikingly pretty on a normal day; tonight, with her hair upswept, touches of makeup, and a midnight blue dress trimmed with snowy lace that Ellie had not seen before, she looked positively radiant.

"I suspect you'll have a number of dance partners this evening," Ellie teased as they huddled together against the whipping wind. She'd worn her regular boater hat, though her own upswept hair might be suffering for it. No matter. The Worth gown was extravagant enough; her hair didn't need to appear pristine too.

"Oh, goodness, I hope not," Audrey moaned.

They turned along Canyon Avenue, following a few others who were on their way toward the church. The moon had risen in a clear sky, though a few last ribbons of pale blue and pink lingered near the peaks of the snow-capped twin mountains.

"Why not?" Ellie asked, though she anticipated the answer. Audrey took a moment to reply and when she did, confirmed Ellie's theory.

"The only dance partner I've ever wanted, and will ever want, was George. No, I'll be happy to watch *you* fending off all your potential dance partners," she said with a laugh. Ellie could tell she wanted to move on from the topic; that the memory of her husband would only threaten to derail the merriness of the evening.

The church with its tall windows of honeyed, shining light and its front door trimmed with garland came into view. Muffled violin music played within the church, and glass hurricane lanterns and punched tin lamps trimmed the shoveled path to the front steps. The glowing path teased at warmth, and Ellie and Audrey walked faster.

"You know, I only wore this gown for Bobby and Graham Booker," Ellie said, shivering, though not only from the cold. Why nerves had suddenly attacked her she couldn't say. Was it really just the showy gown? As the stiff wooden steps creaked under their weight, Ellie allowed the truth a foothold—she'd been ignoring it all evening. All week, in fact.

"Mary Booker's boys?" Audrey said. They entered the church, and instant, overwhelming heat and chatter greeted them.

Coats and cloaks and scarves and hats had been hung on a rack, and as Ellie shed her heavy coat and hat, she didn't have the courage to look around the church. Instead, she pretended she wasn't at all nervous to see Jack. He'd come to McClure's once after returning from Grantstown, just to make sure she was well and to assure her that Hodge had been taken to a doctor for treatment. Jack hadn't stayed, however, even when Audrey offered him a plate of piping hot shepherd's pie. The awkwardness between him and Ellie had felt a little like opposing magnets.

"Ellie?" Audrey interrupted her troubled thoughts. "You said something about the Booker boys?"

She blinked and focused on Audrey again. "Oh, yes," she said, smoothing down the waist of her dress. A handful of people around her turned their heads to look at her gown, eyebrows going up and lips popping open. She tried to ignore them.

"Mary said the boys were planning a special surprise for me," she explained, her stomach tight with indecision. Despite Audrey's insistence that she wear the gorgeous gown and show up Muriel and all her unpleasant friends, she wished she'd gone upstairs to her room to change after all.

She swept a glance around the crowded church floor, telling herself she was looking for the Booker family, not Jack. But it was the Booker family who found *her*, and as she caught sight of Bobby and Graham running toward her through the crowd, her nerves scattered like dry leaves in a heavy wind.

"Doc Ellie!" Bobby said as he came to a stop before her. He and his brother were dressed in their Sunday best, and Bobby's flaking rash from the fever had mostly healed. The boys' eyes widened as they gazed up at her, their mother and father coming up behind them, arm-in-arm.

"Bobby, you're looking well," Ellie said. "And you too, Graham. Both of you look like young gentlemen tonight."

They continued to ogle her gown. "You look like a princess," Graham said.

"No, she doesn't," Bobby said, nudging his brother. "She looks like a *queen*."

Ellie fought a laugh at their innocent earnestness, and beside her, Audrey put a hand over her mouth to hide her own laughter.

"Boys," Mary said, reprimanding them, and then gave Bobby a little tap on his shoulder. He sprang to attention and seemed to remember something.

He untied something from his wrist—it looked like a flower corsage—and then held it out to Ellie. Though her bodice was a little tight in the ribs, she lowered herself into a crouch, coming face to face with the young boys. She let Bobby place the corsage in her hand, and with increasing wonder, realized that it wasn't a real flower, but one made of cut paper. Red, green, and white pieces of paper had been meticulously cut and arranged into the appearance of a blooming rose. The paper rose had then been fastened to a strip of silk ribbon with a bit of wire and glue.

"My goodness, boys," she said as her eyes grew hazy. "I don't think I've ever seen anything so beautiful. Did you make this?"

Bobby and Graham nodded proudly, and with good reason. They had to have spent a long time cutting out the petals and arranging them just so.

"I must say that this is the most creative present I've ever received," she said, running her fingers over the paper petals.

Bobby shoved his brother aside when Graham tried to take it from her hand.

"I'm just going to put it on her!" Graham argued.

"No, I am!" Bobby shouted.

Mr. Booker shook his head and put a hand on both of his son's shoulders. "Boys, how about we let our new sheriff do the honors?"

Ellie snapped her chin up, but it wasn't Deputy Munns who had joined them. It was Jack. *New sheriff?* She straightened her legs and gaped at the shiny gold badge pinned to his suit coat. He grinned and held out his hand.

"Need help with that?" he asked.

Ellie realized after a belated moment that he meant the paper corsage. She fumbled to give it to him, her mind still racing as Jack circled her gloved wrist with the ribbon and tied off the ends so that the corsage fit snugly.

Ellie touched the paper petals and then leaned forward to kiss the tops of Bobby and Graham's heads. "I will treasure this," she told them, and she meant every word. The paper rose was worth more to her than hundreds of kerchiefs filled with coins.

"I think such gallantry deserves a reward," Audrey said, holding out her hands to the boys. "Caleb and Maggie have the dessert table set up near the back. Let's go have a look, shall we?"

She gave Ellie an encouraging and mischievous wink before leading the Booker family straight through the crowd, toward the refreshments table, and leaving her and Jack very much alone.

Still touching the paper petals, Ellie turned to him. "Sheriff, is it?"

His nonchalant shrug didn't convince her. "The governor sent a telegram this afternoon, offering me the job."

"But Deputy Munns…?"

"Is perfectly happy as deputy," Jack said, with another unconvincing shrug. Ellie had questioned whether Munns would truly make an affective sheriff. He was a good man, but he simply didn't have that authoritative edge to him that Jack did.

"You don't look happy about it," she said, then ventured a guess at his reluctance. "Did you not want the position?"

He looked out into the crowd of townsfolk, some dancing in the middle of the church as a pair of fiddles played, and others standing in small groups, holding cups of punch.

"After my badge was taken, I worked real hard to convince

myself I didn't want to be sheriff anyhow," he said, still watching the people around them. "But the truth was, I did—and I'd just failed at it. I'd failed this town and the people, and well, doc...I'm not sure I deserve this badge back."

He met her stare, surprising her with this raw piece of honesty.

"Jack," she said, shaking her head. "Everyone in Sage Canyon believes in you. You've never stopped being their sheriff, not really. Payton was the one who let them down, not you."

Jack had been there without hesitation when Frank was killed, and when Hank Jerrick was shot. He'd gone with her to Grantstown, tried to arrange a deal with Marshal Bevins on Tom's behalf, and organized a posse when Ellie was taken too.

However, she suspected the guilt Jack had buried himself with, layer by layer, the last few years would take time to brush away. Guilt over his behavior after his wife was killed; over having his badge taken; over his feelings for Ellie, even. Guilt weighed unbearably heavy at times. Ellie knew that firsthand.

She laid her hand on his arm. He needed a friend's reassurance, and she would be that friend. He'd been clear about his heart not being ready to move on from Sarah, and Ellie would respect that.

"I'm glad you're wearing that badge," she said.

He exhaled and gave a reluctant grin. Then, a moment later, it spread into something more roguish. "Not as glad as I am that you're wearing that dress."

Ellie dropped her hand from his arm, but not before giving it a playful shove.

"Honest, doc, that is one helluva fine dress." He was finished with their serious discussion about being sheriff, and Ellie grudgingly relented.

"Thank you," she said, a self-conscious swirl working its way through her as once again she smoothed the satin silk at her waistline.

The quartet of fiddlers seated near the refreshments table had paused after the last notes of the previous song, leaving Jack's compliment and her reply hanging in the suddenly empty air. But then, a slow strain of music started up again. Jack held out his hand to her.

"Care to dance with your sheriff, ma'am?"

Grateful that his humor had lightened the moment, she slid her hand into his. They moved into the middle of the church, where a few other couples were dancing. It wasn't a waltz or anything ballroom official, just a piece of fiddle music to slowly sway to. Jack rested a hand on her hip while she laid hers on his shoulder, and their other hands joined together, extended at their sides. Though they stood close, their bodies didn't touch.

"You know," she said, needing to speak, if only to fill the space between them. "I was proud of you, when you let Chet Hodge be taken in alive."

He grunted, as if in contention. "You shouldn't be. If he hadn't already been dying of sepsis, I'd have put a bullet in him."

She sucked in a breath, startled by the fire in his voice. "What have you heard from Grantstown?"

Hodge's condition had been on her mind the last handful of days. She felt pity for him in some ways, and in others, nothing but anger.

"Bevins sent word. Hodge passed just like you said he would," Jack answered.

The dip in Ellie's stomach didn't make much sense. The man had been an outlaw. A heartless killer. And yet, she would have rather he spend the rest of his days in jail than die.

"And Payton?" she asked.

"In Denver—for real this time. He'll be charged with murder, and his confession will likely mean a short trial."

They spun slowly around the other couples. Every few moments, a view of the dessert table appeared over Jack's shoulder. Caleb and Maggie stood shoulder to shoulder there, whispering back and forth in their own conversation. Their cheeks were pink, smiles bashful. They were young and so sweet on each other. It seemed so uncomplicated. Ellie found herself a little envious.

"What are you grinning at?" Jack asked, peering down at her. "Payton's demise?"

"No!" she exclaimed, then lowered her voice as the couple next to them—Mr. Yeaton and his wife—glanced her way. "I'm not sorry he's going to prison—"

"Neither am I. The bastard abducted you, and if what Nate told me is true, he would've killed you too." Jack's tone had gone stone cold somber. He waited for her to say something, and reluctantly, she nodded.

"Mr. Walker saved my life," she admitted.

Jack's fingers tensed around her hand, then relaxed. Maybe it was just her imagination, but he also seemed to tug her a little closer on their next shuffle step.

Ellie cleared her throat. "You did what you set out to do. Justice has been served for Sarah's death and Mr. Toft's injury. Is your mind at east at all, now that Hodge is gone?"

Jack loosened his grip. Ellie breathed easier now that they weren't standing so close. She wondered if that wasn't the result she'd intended for.

"It's funny. Justice doesn't feel like I thought it would. My mind is at rest," he said, but then, meeting her eyes briefly, added, "I'm not sure yet about my heart."

Everything that had transpired with Chet Hodge and his gang —his capture and death—had given Jack the vengeance he'd so desperately wanted. But none of that could bring Sarah back, and it appeared he still wasn't ready to let go. Oddly enough, instead of a slap of disappointment, Ellie felt only resignation. And understanding.

The fiddle music came to a stop. All around them, other couples parted and moved from the dance floor talking and laughing boisterously. The commotion made it a little less awkward as she and Jack did the same.

"Can I get you some punch?" he asked.

Ellie gave a smile and nod, unexpectedly grateful to have a moment to herself, and he slipped between the Yeatons, toward the refreshments table. She let out a long breath and again, ran her fingers over the paper rose corsage. Inside her silk gloves, her palms felt warm and a little slick. Goodness, why was she so unsettled?

"*Hem, hem,*" a throat cleared behind her. The sound had the effect of fork tines scraping up her spine, and Ellie spun around.

Mayor Carson and his wife stood before her; the mayor wore a discomforted expression as he adjusted his tie, and Muriel peered down her thinned nostrils at Ellie. Her eyes swept over the Worth gown. Katherine had once told her that Muriel and her friends traveled to Grantstown, and sometimes even Denver, to shop for their dresses. Ellie cut a quick look to the dessert table, where Audrey was watching with a gleam of satisfaction.

"Miss Lennox," the mayor began, "we were relieved to hear that you were returned to Sage Canyon unharmed."

Ellie stopped a quizzical expression from fully forming on her face. *Returned to Sage Canyon?* Put that way, she sounded like an errant package lost by the U.S. Postal Service.

"Well…thank you," she said, curious and a bit skeptical.

"We also wish to express our gratitude for what you did for the children sickened by scarlet fever," he added stiffly. She gritted her teeth against an amused grin. The words were so stiff, they'd clearly been practiced. They seemed to pain him greatly too.

"I was happy to be of help," she replied, still guardedly.

"Yes, well, Mr. Roberts hasn't yet been successful in hiring a physician for the miners and their family, so it very well may be that they will have to seek treatment through you this winter," he said, sounding more appropriately bitter now.

Ellie only grinned. "They know where to find me."

The mayor grunted and, turning on his heel, started away. Though her arm was hooked around her husband's, Muriel hesitated a moment, her attention still perusing Ellie's gown.

"Muriel how is your ankle?" she asked, remembering her fall on the mercantile steps and how she'd stubbornly refused treatment.

She snapped her eyes up and flared them. "Perfectly fine, *thank you.*"

"You're very welcome," Ellie replied, thoroughly enjoying the blaze of irritation on the woman's face as she hastened away.

As she made her way toward the outer edges of the main floor, the pews having been cleared away once more as they'd been for the bake sale, Ellie felt the phantom press of eyes on her back. Her skin, bared by the V-shape of the bodice, tingled between her shoulder blades. It wasn't unlike the intuitive sensation of someone sneaking up behind her. It took every ounce of grace she possessed—which she usually sorely lacked—to not spin around. A part of her already knew who she would see when she finally, leisurely, and tactfully, turned toward the church entrance.

Henry had arrived. And he wasn't alone.

CHAPTER 19

*H*enry towered over the flock of townsfolk arriving at the dance. His eyes met Ellie's as he was helping Katherine Toft out of her cranberry-colored coat. It appeared that they had come together.

Ellie averted her attention, pretending as to look for someone. Jack, of course. He *was* getting her punch. He was still by the table, caught in conversation. The town was happy to have their sheriff back and surely wanted to offer him congratulations. Ellie, selfishly, wished he would excuse himself and come back with the drinks, if only so that she wouldn't be standing alone.

But that was wrong of her, she knew. She should want Jack to be at her side for a better reason than that. The fact that she didn't—and that Henry's arrival with Katherine pricked like a needle—made her question everything.

Was she being capricious? No longer wanted by Jack, had she simply latched on to the next possible bachelor? She had never been quick with her affections in the past; the idea of men and romance had fallen far behind education and medicine. However, almost as soon as she'd come to Sage Canyon, she'd started to like

Jack as more than a friend. And almost as quickly, she'd *dis*liked Henry Goodwin.

Had that now changed for the right reasons?

Ellie realized she was frowning when Katherine craned her neck and waved to signal her attention. Katherine's jubilant grin only served to drag Ellie's stomach a little lower—she looked so happy, and Ellie shouldn't have felt even a twinge of jealousy or resentment for that.

"Gracious!" Katherine exclaimed as she hurried forward, her blue eyes, round as dinner plates, pinned on the Worth dress. "Look at you! You're simply stunning."

Ellie flattened her palms against the front of her gown again, self-conscious. Now, more than ever, she wished she'd changed. While everyone else had dressed in their finest, the fashions were still modest.

"It's a little too much," Ellie admitted, finding it easy to be honest with her. Like Audrey, Katherine had become a friend. Which was another reason why she felt so guilty about her reaction to her arrival with Henry.

He had followed Katherine, though with less enthusiasm, and arrived within earshot as Katherine shook her head emphatically. "Not at all! This is the town's biggest party all year long—you're supposed to wear the finest dress you own."

Katherine's was beautiful, too, if a bit dated. It was made of violet chiffon and cream lace trim, with a voluminous skirt and petticoats. She turned to Henry. "Don't you agree, Doctor Goodwin?"

He stuck his hands into his trouser pockets and looked as if he wished to be anywhere but here, being asked his opinion on fashion.

"I feel silly now that I realize I should have worn my finest dress," he said with such solemnity that it took a few moments for Ellie and Katherine to grasp his humor and belt out laughter.

"Oh, Doctor Goodwin, you should really be on stage somewhere," Katherine said, catching her breath.

Henry's expression remained placid, and despite his joke, Ellie suspected he was irritated by something. He didn't respond to Katherine's quip, but she didn't seem to notice. She'd caught sight of someone in the crowd and raised her hand in a wave.

"There's Mrs. Cameron."

Ellie followed her attention toward a woman in a plain green dress across the church. Mrs. Cameron's daughter, Ann, had been one of Ellie's first patients after the little girl had been pinned by a boulder that had come down the mountainside. Ann still walked with a limp, but as she followed her mother toward the dessert table, Ellie noticed it was less pronounced than before.

"Excuse me, I need to let her know about an order she placed," Katherine said, and then darted off, leaving Ellie and Henry.

With a nervous knot forming in the base of her throat, Ellie forced herself to acknowledge him with a glance.

"Doctor Lennox," he greeted.

He'd called her Ellie before. Though, he might have thought it too familiar for a function like this.

"Doctor Goodwin," she replied in kind. "I didn't realize you were coming to Sage Canyon for the dance."

As soon as she said it, Ellie wished to take the inane comment back. Why on earth *would* she have known? As if he'd bother to send her a telegram, announcing his intention.

He kept his hands in his pockets, and the milling crowd had his thorough attention. "I didn't come just for the dance."

"Oh." She had a creeping suspicion. "You're here on business, then?"

The same *business* that brought him to Toft's Mercantile a few times each month.

"Yes." His eyes skipped to where Katherine stood with Mrs. Cameron and Ann. "And I also needed to return Dade's gun. I didn't feel right giving it to Audrey when she returned my case."

Audrey and Maggie had taken the train to Grantstown earlier in the week to visit Fiona and the new baby, and Audrey offered to return the case to Henry while she was there. Ellie had handed over the leather case with mixed feelings—she was both relieved someone else would return it, and disappointed that she wouldn't be the one to do it. She would have been welcome to travel with them, but she'd wanted to stay in town on the off chance one of the children who'd been in quarantine needed her.

The fiddle music had started up again, this time in a quickstep tune.

"Have you heard that Hodge died?" she asked.

Henry finally looked at her; behind his wire spectacles, his eyes burned with loathing. "I did, and considering he held you at the end of his pistol, I can't say I'm sorry he's gone."

The memory of Henry emerging from the trees, holding Dade's revolver at his hip, as if he was an old hat at gunslinging, did something funny to her heart: It thumped wildly, skipped, then jogged to catch up again.

Henry didn't look away. Instead, now that he'd peeled his gaze from the crowd, he seemed to take in a deep breath and hold it. The fiddle music, though still playing, muffled a little as he raked Ellie's figure with a slow sweep of his eyes. It was as if he was looking at her for the first time since entering the church. As if none of Katherine's praise over her gown had ever registered within him.

Her skin flushed, though not just in the usual spots, on her cheeks or the tips of her ears. Heat pushed from her skin everywhere, from her head to her chest to her stomach and legs. When he lifted his gaze to meet hers again, some strange and enigmatic part of her simply knew that they were thinking of the same thing—their near kiss on the bluff.

Flustered, Ellie stammered the beginning of a comment about her paper corsage gift, just as Henry asked, "Is Jack Granger courting you?"

Ellie gaped up at him, shock nearly suffocating her next breath. "I…what?"

More heat engulfed her neck and crept to her face, but Henry remained steadfast. He took a step closer. "I asked if Granger is courting you."

Despite the jubilant fiddling and Henry's lowered voice, his question was clear and loud in her ears. It seemed to vibrate within her very bones. She parted her lips, still stunned.

"Why would you ask that?" she managed to reply. It was abominably brazen. Then again, in the past, Henry had never held back his opinions or questions, no matter how bold.

"I saw the way he looked at you in Grantstown, when he found us outside Doctor Jansen's office." His intense stare faltered, and for a moment he nearly appeared bashful. "And, well…I've heard some rumors that he is."

Ellie glanced at Katherine. She saw her looking and gave a happy wave.

"Katherine told you this?"

Henry went rigid again. "I hope you're not angry. She didn't mean any harm."

"I'm not angry," she said, fully aware of her snapping tone.

Henry cocked his head. "Could've fooled me."

Mortified by her brash reaction, Ellie felt heat suffuse her cheeks again. Gracious, she was tired of the way her body kept betraying her; she didn't know what to feel or think about anything it seemed. Henry's question perplexed her, though. And for Ellie, that wouldn't stand.

She set her chin. "Are you asking because you nearly kissed me on the bluff?"

Anyone else might have been bowled over by such a forth-right question. Not Henry, though. No, he had to go and issue an argument: "You nearly kissed me right back."

Her eyes burned with sudden, unmitigated insult. "I'll have you know, Doctor Goodwin, that I don't kiss men who are already spoken for. And I certainly don't court one man and let another kiss me. Now if you'll excuse me." With her pulse spiking, she turned on her heel for the desserts table.

She hadn't taken three steps before she spotted Jack cutting through the crowd, transporting two cups of punch carefully, so as not to spill either. Heedless of what she was doing or where she was going, Ellie broke off in the other direction. The loud fiddling and laughter, the press of shoulders and skirts, booming voices, and wide grins as she wove between people threatened to suffocate her, and then before she knew it, she was darting out the front doors of the church and reveling in the freedom of the night air. She drew in deep gulps of it, furious, both with Henry and with herself.

No sooner had she descended from the last step than the first wallops of humiliation struck. *Why* couldn't she control herself around that man? It seemed she was either sniping at him or completely losing her composure in his arms.

"Ellie!" Henry's voice chased her down the lantern-lit pathway. Her legs gummed up and she groaned as she slowed to a stop. Still, she couldn't bring herself to face him, even when his boots crunched to a halt on the snowpack right behind her.

Something warm and heavy touched down onto her shoulders, and after an initial burst of surprise, she realized it was her coat. She'd left the church without it, and now, Henry draped it over her. She pulled the collar closer, belatedly realizing how cold she'd been without it.

"Look at me, Ellie," he murmured. There was no challenge, no aggravation in his tone now. With a defeated sigh, she turned and hitched her chin. He brought his cupped hands to his mouth and blew warm breath into them. He wasn't wearing his jacket, and yet he'd thought to bring hers.

"What did you mean when you said you don't kiss men who are spoken for?" he asked.

She looked heavenward; the night sky was riddled with stars, and for some reason, they seemed so much closer than ever before.

"Katherine Toft," she said softly.

"Miss Toft?" He rubbed his palms together to create friction and heat. Abruptly, he stopped. "Oh. You think…that she and I…"

Ellie peered at him with dawning regret. Henry's wide grin and bark of amusement solidified it.

"Why are you laughing?" she demanded.

"I'm not courting Miss Toft," he said, still grinning like a fox.

Inside her stomach, a shiver of confusion twined around one of relief. "But your business in Sage Canyon…every time you visit, you go to the mercantile to see her."

"I'm there to see *Mr.* Toft, not Katherine."

Ellie pulled back, taking a long, serious look at Henry. "Barry Toft?"

He frowned. "He asked that my visits be kept quiet."

"But…why? What are the visits for?"

"Therapy, to help him regain some function in his legs. It's just an experiment." He held up his hands to stop her from cutting in with questions. "Katherine had written to my pharmacy over the summer. She had seen her father's legs and feet twitching when he moved around in his wheeled chair, and it led her to wonder if his paralysis is really permanent, or if maybe he was healing, albeit slowly."

Ellie stared at him, astonished. "She never mentioned it to me. I wanted to meet Mr. Toft and see if there might be anything I could do to help, but she said he…well, that he refused to see me."

Shame pulled the last few words low in her throat so that they were barely audible.

"He doesn't trust physicians," Henry said. "I'm sure if he met you, he'd change his mind, but he's a stubborn old goat."

She couldn't pretend that Mr. Toft's refusal to see her didn't sting, but her stoked curiosity helped her quickly recover. "What kind of therapy is it?"

"I've been trying to stimulate his nerves using small electrical currents, increasing in strength and frequency as we progress."

Electrical currents. Ellie blinked, astonished. "Has it had any effect?"

"Possibly. He's regaining some feeling in one of his feet, but it might not have anything to do with the therapy. It could simply be natural recovery."

The idea was intriguing to say the least. She wondered how he'd come to think of it. "It's quite out of the realm of pharmacology," she said.

Speaking about the therapy, he'd become animated, his expression opening with interest. Now, he tempered it with a reserved grimace. "I couldn't find any medicine that might help."

"So, you thought of electrical currents?"

"A physician from Harvard wrote a case study."

"I see," she murmured, impressed by such innovation. There was much more to Doctor Goodwin than she'd given him credit for. "So...you haven't been going to the mercantile because you like Katherine."

My goodness, she felt a fool now. If the air hadn't been so cold, she might have even started to blush.

"I like Miss Toft just fine." Henry came a step closer. "But it's you I can't stop thinking about."

Ellie stared at him, breathless, her lips gaping. "I...but I didn't think you liked me very much," she said weakly.

He replied with a slow, sly grin. "I didn't. At first."

Things had changed. For them both, it seemed. She tried to pin down when she had started feeling anticipation rather than dread upon seeing Henry Goodwin.

The few times she'd spied him on Main Street over the last couple of months, her curiosity had led her to think about him more. Had it been then? Certainly, when he arrived in Sage Canyon with the antiserum and insisted on staying, she'd felt a peculiar and new awareness of him. And the pointed longing for him to discover that she was in danger, and to find her in the forest with Payton and Hodge had been potent.

The moon drifted out from behind a strip of clouds and glinted off his spectacles. Unable to see his eyes behind the gleam, she looked to his mouth as he asked, once again, "Are you courting Jack?"

"No." To her wonder, the answer wasn't accompanied by pang of disappointment. Rather, as Henry touched her cheek, his fingertips warm despite the frigid air, she felt fortunate that she wasn't spoken for.

"I'd like to kiss you, Ellie."

"You would?" she whispered. He smiled at her breathless question, said Ellie shook herself from her daze. "I mean to say... ah...yes?"

Before more amusement could cross his lips, she rose onto her toes and pressed her mouth to his. Her boldness shocked her just as much as it seemed to shock him. He gripped her shoulders and drew her firmly against him, kissing her in return. Wonder and warmth spread through her, tricking her body into thinking the sun had emerged or perhaps a great bonfire had just been touched off directly behind her.

Ellie savored the feel of his kiss, of the curl of electric pleasure jolting through her. It made no sense how this brooding, blunt, and oftentimes infuriating man could make her feel uncharacteristically out of control. Her mind, usually so practical and logical, now churned with turbulent desires, all of which were heedless of propriety and restraint. The firm grip he kept on her, the easy way he lifted her to the very tips of her toes and held her aloft, so that she was hardly standing on her own at all anymore, only threw more kindling into the inferno building within her.

The chill night stole across her lips when the kiss broke off, and Ellie dragged in a gasping breath. Her eyelids were heavy and her mouth a bit numb when she murmured, "I don't understand what's happening."

His soft chuckle seemed to reverberate all the way through her. "It's called a kiss, Doctor Lennox."

Sobered by his teasing tone, Ellie dropped her heels back onto the snow. Restricted by his close hold, she could barely move her arm in order to land a playful smack against his side. All she felt was hard muscle, and she suddenly wished had kept her hands to herself.

"Very amusing," she said, suppressing a grin.

Slowly, as if reluctant to do so, Henry released her, though he remained much closer than was appropriate. There was no one around them on this candlelit path, thank goodness. Everyone had gone into the church, where the music was still playing, and muffled laughter and voices could be heard.

Unexpectedly timid, Ellie cleared her throat and tucked a strand of hair behind her rather numb ear. The clear moonlight could do nothing to obscure Henry's ardent gaze. Ellie had the startling realization that she had no idea how a man like Henry would conduct himself in matters of attraction. In matters of medicine, and even in matters of daring action, he'd shown her what to expect of him. But this was unchartered territory. What would he expect now that she had kissed him?

Ellie couldn't summon the nerve to ask so direct a question. It concerned her, this timid faltering. She had always been direct to the point of being brash.

"Are you, ah," she began, struggling to speak without shivering, "staying the night in Sage Canyon?"

Instantly, she regretted the question. Considering the last train to Grantstown left hours ago, he would have no choice.

He crossed his arms, tucking in his hands to warm them. "Audrey said she'd have a room."

A small spark zipped through her. Audrey had failed to mention anything at all about inviting Henry Goodwin to spend the night at McClure's. Knowing he'd be sleeping under the same roof that night gave her a disturbing sort of thrill. What in the world was wrong with her?

"You're freezing," Ellie said, watching him as he shuffled from foot to foot. "We should go back inside."

Being around others might also eliminate the urge to kiss him again.

She took a step toward the church, but Henry caught her arm. "Do you want to dance?"

Her heart tripped at the request. Dance. With Henry. A fleeting image of him holding her close again as they twirled around the dance floor accompanied the distant, soft strains of a waltz.

"You're determined to fluster me this evening, aren't you?" she said with a huff of laughter. *There.* That frankness was more like it.

Henry grinned, his hand still gently clutching her elbow. "Just this evening?"

"I didn't take you as a dancer," she said, refusing to rise to his teasing.

With a tug, he easily brought her into position before him, one hand on her hip, the other lacing her fingers. She gaped. "What, *here*?"

"You're right, I'm not a dancer," he said as Ellie set her hand on his shoulder. "I wouldn't mind a little practice before we go back inside."

The excuse to be alone a while longer charmed rather than vexed her.

"Very well, Doctor Goodwin, but if you develop a case of frostbite, I'm afraid I'll have to take you directly to my infirmary."

Without warning, he spun her around, her feet leaving the ground as her sharp crack of surprise echoed into the night. Henry set her back down again and launched into a waltzing step. "Dually noted, Doctor Lennox," he murmured.

As the narrow, shoveled path became their private dance floor, Ellie marveled at her unexpected dance partner. How Henry had become this source of warmth and light and fascination still bewildered her, but Ellie was coming to understand that her life in Colorado would never be predictable. It was one of the many reasons why Sage Canyon and its people were becoming so dear to her. She'd already started to treasure this wild place and all it offered, no matter how challenging or dangerous or baffling.

The cold didn't seem to reach them at all as they moved in time with the fiddle music, bursting out in laughter when Henry's heel knocked over a lantern and when Ellie trampled his toes. The pair of them weren't perfect in the least. Life rarely was, either. The trick, she was coming to learn, was to hold on tight and meet whatever came next with squared shoulders and a determination to do something good.

And for as long as she could, Ellie planned to do just that.

THANK YOU

I hope you enjoyed A CURE IN THE WILD! I've loved continuing Doc Ellie's adventures in Sage Canyon, and I hope to keep writing more. Reader reviews can ensure that! They make a huge impact on a book's success, so I hope you'll take a moment to leave a rating and review. Thank you!

ALSO BY CARA DEVLIN

THE TROUBLE WE KEEP

A Second Chance Western Romance

———————

A HEART WORTH HEALING

(Sage Canyon Book 1)

ABOUT THE AUTHOR

Cara is an author, history lover, and Netflix junkie. She loves to read and write across genres, but her heart is reserved for adventurous and romantic historical fiction. When she's not writing, she's either freelance editing, driving her kids everywhere, burning at least one side of a grilled cheese, or avoiding doing the laundry.

Printed in the USA
CPSIA information can be obtained
at www.ICGtesting.com
LVHW092326200324
775081LV00032B/674